To Ina

Enjoy

N. Shepherd

(Vinny)

CRYSTA

N. Shepherd

AuthorHouse™ UK Ltd.
500 Avebury Boulevard
Central Milton Keynes, MK9 2BE
www.authorhouse.co.uk
Phone: 08001974150

© 2010 N. Shepherd. All rights reserved.

No part of this book may be reproduced, stored in a retrieval system, or transmitted by any means without the written permission of the author.

First published by AuthorHouse 4/5/2010

ISBN: 978-1-4490-7073-1 (sc)

This book is printed on acid-free paper.

This book is dedicated to all the Heroes' that have fought, those that have died and especially for those that are still fighting. Come home safe!

10% of the proceeds from the sale of each book will be donated to Help the Heroes.

Author's Notes:

I would like to mention my sister T.C as she was the first person to read Crysta. This is a big deal as she would never normally read anything that is more than four sentences long. So not only did she choose to read it, off her own back, but she completed it and liked it too. Not that she has many books to compare mine too, but still it's nice. Also it is her artistic genius that illustrates the front cover. With two kids and a husband, I really appreciate her finding the time. Thanks loads, I love it.

Thanks to my husband Andy for supporting me in the writing of this book. When I lost my entire first attempt, because my laptop took it into whatever world laptops swallow important work into, he was the one who insisted that I start again. He has yet to read this book, as I haven't written the kind of story that he likes, but it's appreciated that he's backed me anyway.

To my wonderful parents for their encouragement in not just the writing of this book but in everything I do. I know it's part of the job description but still, thanks.

Also a shout out to all my friends who said some top stuff when they found out I was getting the book published. Remember you all promised to buy one.

CHAPTER ONE

Let me tell you about a woman called Crysta. Crysta Sloane is about 5ft 3 and a bit, long brown hair, pretty ordinary looking, and she works for the Devil. Well it seemed a good idea at the time. You see what happened was, she got hit by a car and an agent that worked for the Devil offered Crysta a deal to work for his boss and in return she would carry on living. Her job would be to convert people to worship Satan. When she looked at her body that had been chucked a few feet into the road, after bouncing off the window screen, Crysta made the decision that she wanted to live so she accepted the offer. Besides she always figured that when she died she would go to hell anyway, because all her friends would be there. As it worked out when she did actually die they weren't there yet because she was a few decades early. She was only seventeen when it happened. So she thought at least now she has the best seats in the Hell reserved for when she goes there for real. Crysta had been doing the job about ten years now and hadn't managed to convert anyone. She joined the Army instead.

As part of the welcome package they gave Crysta the ability to kill people. In fact this was the only ability they ever gave you. They didn't vary it month to month or give a list of options like:-

Which of the following abilities would you like?

- A. Fly
- B. Read minds
- C. Teleport
- D. Kill things
- E. None of the first three as they aren't real options but it was fun messing with you.

This was the reason Crysta joined the Army. She reasoned that should she be sent to a war zone and run out of bullets she would still be ok. There was no skill involved, no pointing the finger at them and a bolt of lightning would strike whoever she was pointing at dead, nope nothing cool like that. Not even a magic word like Die or Have it. No, all Crysta had to do was just think them dead and really want it and they would be well, dead. Some of Crysta's ex boyfriends had no idea how close they'd come to being worm food. The fact none of them actually died meant that deep down Crysta obviously didn't mean it, despite how much she thought she did. So never having been in a position to use this skill for real she wasn't sure that if a ton of Taliban did happen to be heading towards her and she had run out of bullets, whether her skill would actually work on more than one person at a time and perform quick enough to save her ass. She hoped that she would never have to find out.

The only things Crysta had used her 'power' on so far were the occasional fly or daddy long legs that happened to be buzzing around her room when she was trying to sleep and some stinging nettles that were overgrown on a path she wanted to walk down while taking her dog Prince out for a walk and she couldn't be bothered to turn around and take a different route.

Prince was a German shepherd. I mean she wasn't going to own a Doberman like Damian in the Omen, how stereotypical would that be? Some things however are a given. Like posh people who live in the country, that own a Landrover, wear wax jackets and have at least one Labrador. If they owned a poodle it just wouldn't be right. Sometimes it's got to fit for the mind to accept it as normal. Well Crysta didn't want to be normal and get a Doberman. Firstly, people didn't know she worked for the Devil so they didn't expect her to have one anyway and secondly Prince was a family dog and he was around way before this whole working for the Devil came about.

Actually that part about people not knowing wasn't technically true. Crysta had told her older (by two years) and only other sibling about it, a week after it happened. Her sister at the time was into Heavy Metal music and her walls were covered in posters of people with straggly hair and skeletons. Her sister Sky (the parents weren't in fact all that much into flower power, but when you give your kids names like that it's what you think) Sky, after telling people her name, was used to the question of "oh your parents were hippies then?" or something similar, when she would reply "No." a flash of confusion would cross over the person's face. Sometimes she would say, "My name is Sky but no my parents weren't into smoking dope." If they didn't actually say it Sky knew they were thinking it. Her parents just liked the name and didn't think of the future implications for naming their daughter Sky and not even having the courtesy of being hippies so Sky could justify it.

Anyway, like I said, Sky was into Heavy Metal and most of those sorts of songs were about Crysta's new Boss. Then she thought it was totally cool that her little sister worked for the Dark lord. Crysta even killed a spider for her once because her sister was worried she would swallow it in her sleep if it came to drink her saliva from her mouth. This happens and Crysta found she slept better if she didn't think about it and did a thorough search of her room first. As time had gone on and they grew up, her sister asked her less and less about it, and they never mentioned it any more. It was just easier that way. The adult brain sometimes just can't cope with the abnormal.

CHAPTER TWO

Despite what people think God actually created the dog first! It was a collie. Then he created a garden for the dog to run around in and do its business. He named it Dog because it was a play on God. Why make things difficult if they can be made easy. While God was creating he found naming things the hardest so the simpler the better. He realised that the whole world couldn't just be a garden with dog in it, and a tree for dog to cock his leg up against. So before he went off to finish his planet and try and name things, he created Man. His job was to look after dog by throwing apples for him. He had added them to the tree because dog liked to chase and chew them. Man was told he wasn't allowed to eat the apples as they were for dog and left.

When he returned, Man had an abnormally muscled right arm from throwing apples, God assumed. Man declared he was bored and even though Dog was good company he couldn't speak and he and wanted someone to talk too. Also he told God he wanted to be called Adam. So God made a woman that Adam named Eve. God thought long and hard about adding the breasts. He decided that as they were only wearing leaves then the top half should look different. He then thought that he would take away the dangly thing for Eve because it looked messy and ugly. God had to admit Eve was an improvement and maybe he had rushed Adam a bit.

Adam and Eve were told to look after dog and the garden and not to eat the apples but could eat whatever else they grew or made. It was really hit and miss back then, as Adam and Eve didn't know the difference between edible plants and grass. Despite the warning not to eat the apples one day they did. The apples looked much nicer than anything they'd ever been able to make. When God returned and asked them why they did it they told him a snake told them to do it. As God hadn't yet created a snake he didn't believe them. He kicked them out of the garden, but not before he made them clean it up. This was by the way, way before shovels or poo bags were invented. God later found out that the Devil had placed the snake there. All things had to have an opposite so Satan came about the same time as God. The details of when and how they came about are a bit blurry but from day one they were in constant competition with each other.

So God had created a dog, the Devil the fox. It was more cunning and didn't rely on people to look after it. God created the hamster so the Devil contributed the rat for the same reason as the fox. When God made the Guinea pig the Devil didn't even bother creating anything to trump it as it was basically an overgrown hamster anyway, and the rat beat them both. God, believe it or not, invented the slug for the birds to eat. The Devil therefore made the snail. He found it amusing that any animal that ate them would have to work harder to eat it because he added the shell. The snack however was much smaller. He had a twisted mind really.

The cat was one of the Devils as well. That's why the baddie in a film is normally stroking a cat. Why it's generally a white cat I have no idea. People helped also. God had started with a Collie but now there were many breeds of dog that were bred to help people do various things. God wasn't too impressed when the Chinese bred the Chihuahua just to eat, but he rationalised that when you create a race that is supposed to live on rice, then you can't blame them when the start eating anything.

Between them, God and the Devil had laid the foundations and the planet had spread and developed without any major contribution needed from either of them for hundreds of years. They were getting bored and the rivalry between them was getting stale.

God had been watching Crysta for a long time. Crysta was meant to be met by one of his cherubs first before one of the Devils agents. The Cherub was late because he had been kept behind for extra choir practice as he sang a line wrong from 'Oh come all ye faithful'. God was less than amused but because of who he was, he had to forgive him. In his head he wanted to pluck his wings off but luckily no one knew what he thought a lot of the time.

Crysta had only tried once to convert someone. She asked a guy who was high on drugs, if he wanted to sign his soul over to the Devil. The experience of a girl, who in the eyes of the crack head had horns and red eyes, asking him to join the Devil, was enough to put him on the straight and narrow. So now he now worshipped God. Crysta's fringe line did occasionally curl up into what looked like horns (nothing a strong hair gel couldn't cope with) but the red eyes were definitely something the crack head saw in his drug-addled mind.

So Crysta had converted one person over to him but none to the Devil. Crysta was definitely working for the wrong side. Ok he had to admit she never went to church except to go to friends' weddings, christenings or Remembrance Day.

God could live with that. Church was a drag anyway and he could understand why most people didn't go. It was all long speeches from books that had stories in that were mostly exaggerated by the people who wrote them. Matthew, Luke and John had a lot to answer for once they got to Heaven. God didn't like people who went for fame and exposure over the truth. Hardly anyone knew the words to the hymns and it always sounded awful. Except Gospel singers they had it right but the preachers were way over the top. No Crysta should be working for him and he had to figure out how he was going to get her. The Devil only got her first because his agent was more punctual, so he had her by default really.

CHAPTER THREE

Crysta was quite shocked at how Hell actually looked when she got called there. The Devil, or Boss as she now called him would slow down time in real world and he would page her and she would step out into his office. A kind of screwed up Mr Ben. Crysta couldn't remember if he had ever dressed up as a Devil and stepped out into Hell in one of his cartoons. She doubted it. It was always a cowboy or spaceman costumes. Who would choose to go to Hell? It could be very inconvenient at times. More than once she was on the toilet, or in the shower. Changing rooms in stores, or on a date. On one date the Boss forgot to slow things down. The date thought Crysta had gone to the toilet and made a run for it. When she did get back to the restaurant and realised what happened she felt awful. She had seen him around the camp a few times after but didn't have to the guts to apologise. It wasn't like she could tell him what really happened. He was too short for her anyway. Any bloke shorter than 5ft 2 was definitely out. Crysta just went for the free meal and a break from the block.

Crysta was sat in the Bosses plush office. It was large; the carpet was a deep pile maroon. His desk was an intricately carved oak table that had a laptop sat open on it. Top of the range of course. A tray with two levels. One saying IN, the other OUT. Crysta suspected it was made of real gold. Nothing in his office was cheap. Your average filing cabinet was normally a metal stack with drawers. The Devil had an ornate chest of drawers, again made of oak, which had been made especially for the job. His chair was a huge black leather recliner with fitted massage settings and a cup holder in one of the arms. It had a drawer in the side that was a chiller and it held at max four cans at a time. Her boss always liked to have his supply of Appletiser in there. He had always liked Apples ever since he had been able to get Adam and Eve to eat one; it was his first win over the git upstairs. His words not hers.

When you looked out of the window that stretched across one wall it looked down on the work floor. There were row upon row of desks, all identical. The Devil played out heavy metal music over the tannoy, mainly the ones that were about him or Hell. He didn't like it much, it gave him a headache, but it was supposed to inspire the workers. Highway to Hell was currently playing. The office was air-conditioned but all the surrounding living quarters weren't, so people were always going ill. The genius part, which the Devil prided himself on, was that he wouldn't let anyone take sick leave. Well it is Hell.

The majority of people that ended up in Hell that Crysta noticed were your usual murderers and general other horrid people and of course traffic wardens, fashion designers, Estate Agents and Lawyers. It was normally divorce lawyers. The ones that got old rich men to hand over half of their fortune to some twenty year old gold digger who they thought really loved them. Crysta had no sympathy for these men. I mean they are mostly old, fat and balding. Yeah it's love you idiot not your money at all…..purleese.

The Devil himself was always immaculately dressed. His favourite piece of clothing he had was a black cloak, with a high collar and red velvet lining. He confiscated it off Jack the Ripper once he came down. It billowed out behind him when he walked and made him feel even more powerful somehow. He had heard some of the minions say it made him look a bit like a vampire; he was ok with that. Whatever kept fear in their hearts.

He was wearing a lot of Prada at the moment because he saw a film with the title; the Devil wears Prada and liked the sound of it. He hadn't actually seen it and didn't know it was about a woman fashion editor. Probably best not to tell him. He just had to think of himself in whatever outfit and he would be wearing it. Crysta kept a mental note to ask him how to do it. It would save her a fortune in clothes and she could always be wearing the top labels. Not the stupid catwalk clothes that were completely impractical and the designers charged a fortune for. This was the reason why most of them ended up in Hell. To charge you 200 dollars for a T-shirt that doesn't cover your stomach and drapes over one shoulder so much that your breast falls out. I mean, where would it be acceptable, except maybe Germany, to wear these clothes in public? Ridiculous.

"So what did you page me for this time?" Crysta enquired

"Well Crysta." he replied looking at Crysta with his black pupiless eyes. Crysta had learnt to look at the well-groomed ink black coloured goatee on his face rather than into his eyes. They creeped her out. "I have been looking at my stats." he continued "and you are still my worst agent I have out there. Now tell me why I shouldn't just sack you and turn you into a none living person. I have your soul remember?"

Crysta had heard this speech or a variant of it quite a lot over the years. The first time she freaked and gabbled a million excuses and swore she would try harder. The fact that she hadn't improved and was still around proved that he was all talk and no action. Something, which she didn't know yet, was making him keep her around. Crysta would have been quite flattered and also slightly annoyed if she knew it was because she was being used as a pawn in a, who can get one up on each other between God and her Boss. The Devil knew God wanted her and so he wasn't getting her. It was a principal thing.

"Well you know how it is Boss, I've been busy, there is a war on you know." Crysta stated.

When suicide bombers showed up in Hell, it always shocked them. When they realised that in fact, blowing themselves up, didn't give them an instant fast track to Heaven. No, they came to Hell and the devil had them looking after pigs for eternity. This amused Crysta no end. Her Boss did have a sense of humour at times.

CHAPTER FOUR

Heaven if Crysta ever went there would be exactly as she would have expected. It had the pearly gates, clouds, Angels, Cherubs and good people like Mother Theresa, Einstein, Shakespeare, Elvis and Joan of Ark. God was a traditionalist. He had asked for a retro look once and all that happened was that the pearly gates got painted red and black and when people turned up they thought they had arrived at the back door. This caused St Peter no end of problems so it got put back. Well some things had been improved. The staircase that was just endless up to his office had been replaced with a lift service. There was also an escalator just in case it broke down or if people were claustrophobic. Music was piped into the lift and through speakers that were set at various stages as you ascended on up. Like the Devil, God liked to play songs relating to himself or Heaven in general. His favourite was Stairway to Heaven. No matter which method you took it was still a long trek so not many people went up to his office unless it was absolutely necessary. Everything was done by e-mail. It was quicker. With not much too really do this day and age, God was sending out so many e-mails that St Peter had recruited some cherubs whose only jobs were to read and sort out all his e-mails. They were mostly ones saying things like "keep an eye out for my next important e-mail".

God's office didn't have any walls. It had a white marble desk that looked like it was suspended on nothing. When the sun shone on it, the desk looked translucent and it was easy to walk into. It was also very slippery. When he called files to his desk, if they came in too fast they would just slip straight off again. This is how binder folders got invented.

God got sick of collecting all the papers up when it happened. It never occurred to him to get a different desk. He had a white leather chair with a footrest. It was real leather. He knew some people thought meat was murder. The people however, after he supplied them with animals to eat, realised they could make use of what they couldn't. This, God thought, showed resourcefulness. He had a desk boredom thing. It was the one that you swung out one ball, and it hit against another on the opposite end and it went Click, Clack. The base of it was covered in rubber to stop it slipping off. The base of his keyboard had also been made slip proof and it was attached to a 34inc flat screen monitor. His printer was sat on the opposite corner of his computer but the desk still looked empty. Everything looked vast.

They say when you go to Heaven you see a bright light. This is true. When you go to Hell you see a single red bulb. The Devil isn't one for drama. Neither is God really. The bright light is for health and safety reasons. He doesn't want anyone to trip and hurt themselves on the escalator. As St Peter had pointed out once via e-mail. They are already dead when they get to Heaven so they can't actually hurt themselves. Also the mega watt bulbs, the kind they use at Wembley, were actually blinding people. The fact they couldn't see anything but spots in front of their eyes was the health and safety problem. God refused to change his mind so St Peter had resorted to handing out blackout goggles at the bottom of the stairs.

CHAPTER FIVE

Crysta was on leave and had gone to spend some time with her parents. Currently she was out taking Prince for a walk. Looking out the window the weather looked warm so she had put on some shorts and a T-Shirt. Her legs very rarely got exposed and Crysta wondered whether she should have put up warning posters around the area. They would read something like 'Warning the glare of the sun off this woman's legs because they are so white may cause blindness. For your safety avoid direct staring'. As it worked out it wasn't as warm as it looked but Crysta had gone too far to go back for a jacket even though her arms and legs were now covered in goose bumps. It was early May but the wind still had a chill to it. Crysta had resorted to crossing her arms over her chest. A cold wind does you no favours when you only have a vest T on and no bra.

If I worked for God and not the other one maybe I could do something about the weather' she mused. 'I could have my own personal sun that could follow me around and I'd get a great tan all year round. I guess that would be abusing my powers a bit. Assuming I'd have that power anyway. I'm a good person…aren't I? Ok I've done stupid things but nothing that has ever broken the law. When he asked me if I wanted to work for the Devil and live I didn't really believe it was for real. Not until I got hit by that bloody car, did I really believe in either Heaven or Hell. Well there's nothing like seeing it for real to change your mind. I haven't seen Heaven. I bet God looks just like they portray him in movies. A huge guy, with long white hair and beard that would rival Gandalfs' from Lord of the Rings. I bet he wears those toga looking things that look like dresses as well. I wonder if the Boss could sort me out a day pass so I can have a look around. I'm glad I'm not in Hell permanently and I'm able still to operate up here. All those desks and filing. No windows anywhere, except his, and that looks in. No gardens, trees, flowers. In fact, no outside area at all. Just a huge underground basement. That constant change of temperature from when you're in the work area, then when you leave that room, it's well…it's hotter than Hell. He stole the idea from us though. Earth is an extension of Hell except we're fortunate enough up here to have the fresh air and greenery. Those people that are stuck in air conditioned offices should take the opportunity now to look out the window and away from their computer or leave the office on their break. Make the most of it. I mean how do they know that they aren't going to Hell? I sure as hell didn't.

Crysta was so deep in her thoughts that she hadn't heard Prince barking ahead of her. He was running up and down a spot in the hedge getting excitable. "What is it boy? What have you found?" Crysta ran over to where Prince was desperately trying to scrabble through a small gap in the hedge. Crysta bent down to look through the tightly knit branches and leaves. On the other side she could just make out a small deer. It was lying on its side and his chest was heaving dramatically and it was clearly in pain. Crysta stood up quickly and scanned the length of the hedge in both directions to see if she could find a break where she could get through and help it.

There's got to be a fence or a stile somewhere, come on which way, she thought frantically. She looked right and instincts said try this way first so she broke into a run following the hedge line. Prince was running on just ahead of her. She nearly ran straight past, but set just back in amongst the hedge was a wooden stile. Crysta didn't even climb over but squeezed herself through the gap at the side with Prince trying to get past at the same time. The deer was only about twenty metres away and Crysta started running towards it with Prince barking along beside her.

Suddenly the deer's head came up and it was struggling to try and get to his feet. A feeble sound that sounded like a lamb bleating came from its lips but its injury prevented him from moving but his instincts to run were trying to override it. Crysta realised that it was trying to get away from her so she slowed to a walk. "Prince get here." she half whispered half said. Prince slowed to a trot and looked back at her "Prince come,

come here there's a good lad." Prince hesitated then trotted over to her. "Now you just lay down here and be quiet ok." Prince lay down and Crysta crept slowly forward towards the deer. As she got to the deer Prince was back up into sit but didn't come any closer. The deer had a wild look in its eye. Clearly petrified but had succumbed to the fact he couldn't go anywhere. "Hey, Hey, Hey little man what happened to you?" Crysta asked in soothing tones hoping to calm the deer down. She scanned over him because initially she couldn't see anything wrong. Then she saw it. Wrapped around one of the front legs was a bit of barbed wire. The other front leg she could see had been cut but the wire had caught in the other leg where it must have struggled and had become embedded and the leg was at a peculiar angle. She scanned the field and sure enough across the other side she could see a part of the fence that had been broken. "What did you do? Were you trying to jump the fence running away from something or did you just not see it? You silly thing. You must have landed hard by the looks of that fence then you limped over here and collapsed." Crysta didn't know why she was talking to the deer out loud like this but it was helping her arrange her thoughts and get a grip on the situation.

The deer's head was lying back down again against the grass and the breathing had subsided slightly and it seemed a bit calmer. "You poor, poor thing, don't worry I'll make it ok. Lie still it won't hurt I promise." Crysta closed her eyes and placed a hand on his neck. The coat felt sweaty and clammy and she could feel the pulse weaken. Then he was gone. Crysta had taken his life because she had really wanted him dead. It was the only way she felt that she could really help him. Take away his pain. For a minute she just knelt there next to the deer until Prince came over and snuggled up next to her and was trying to lick her face. He sensed something had happened and wanted to comfort Crysta. "Hey Prince, come on then, there's nothing more I can do now lets go home." The wind was still blowing with a cool air but Crysta could no longer feel it as she took the path back to her parent's house.

CHAPTER SIX

"Oy St Peter, there's a deer at the gate shall I send him to Noahs entrance?" A young Angel yelled over to St Peter. He was being trained up to look after the gate so St Peter could have a break.

"A deer, just now. Hmm I wonder if it's the one." he spoke out loud but was directing it at himself.

"You wonder if it's the one? What do you mean?" St Paul asked

"Hmm, what, oh nothing." St Peter replied realising Paul was still there "One of the cherubs said to look out for a deer that might come to the gate around now. The Guv said something about it in an e-mail and when it gets here, I have to go up and see him."

"Then what?" Paul asked curious

"I don't know, can't believe I've got to go all the way up there. Well send this little guy on to Noah and I suppose I better go and see what this is all about. Watch the gate will you and if those Hells Angels try and get in again lock the gate until I get back ok."

"Yes Sir, will do, no worries." Paul answered with the enthusiasm people have when their in a new job and have been given responsibility for the first time and want to impress the boss.

"Ok good." St Peter replied with slight reservation in his voice and turned and walked towards the lift to the Guv's office. He pressed the button and waited, placing on his sunglasses that he carried on him at all times.

They had put some chairs and magazines out next to the lift to help relieve people's boredom from the wait. If the lift was already at the top it took what felt like forever to come back down. There was also a mirror next to the lift doors. Dr Sigmund Freud had thought of it. He had monitored people and realised that by putting a mirror there people were so distracted by looking at themselves they didn't notice the wait as much. St Peter e-mailed God explaining his concerns about this as it was vanity and vanity was a sin. God replied 'As long as they have stopped moaning I don't care.'

The lift was as fast if not faster than the one that takes you to the top of the Empire State building but you could still spend the best part of a day in it. This was why the lift was actually a small flat. It had a toilet a mini bar with the usual food but non-alcohol refreshment. A huge armchair and 30inch Flat screen TV mounted on the wall with all the channels that had passed the PG sensors. So anything obviously religious was allowed. Even Father Ted and The Vicar of Dibley. The reason these had got through were because the cherubs that did the checking had merely looked at the titles and deemed them worthy of viewing. Some of the contents they would not have approved of. Luckily none of them had figured this out yet, as the channels with these being shown on were the most popular.

When you die you actually don't need the bathroom, need to eat or sleep. The mind refuses to believe this so certain things have stayed. They liked a banquet or two up in Heaven. People still had their rooms with beds in as they kept hold of their trappings of when they truly existed. Funnily enough once they really comprehended that they didn't really have to go to the bathroom despite what the brain told them it was the first thing that they happily stopped doing. Some people just couldn't let it drop so there were bathrooms available just in case.

St Peter had dozed off in the lift chair with a copy of Shakespeare's Taming of the Shrew on his lap. Shakespeare's annual play was a huge deal up in Heaven and even though St Peter auditioned every year he had never got the good parts. He really fancied himself as the Shrews father Baptiste this year. He was pretty sure Marilyn Monroe was going to get the part of the Shrew. He didn't even rate her acting. It was favouritism because she had big breasts and Shakespeare fancied her.

The lifted dinged and came to a halt, jolting St Peter awake. He looked up with half open eyes and realising he had finally reached his destination came to his feet and straightened his robe out. He stepped out into the vastness of near nothingness that was the Guvs office. He was sat behind his desk typing probably more e-mails on his computer.

"Ah Peter, long time no see. What can I do for you? God asked peering down at St Peter through his half moon spectacles. He didn't need glasses but he thought it made him look more amiable. Like Dumbledore from Harry Potter.

"Well Guv you sent an e-mail saying that if a deer showed up at the gate then I was to come up and see you."

"Yes I did, and is the deer here yet? God enquired

No, St Peter thought, I just sat in that lift to come all the way up here to tell you that the deer isn't here yet, but actually said "Yes Guv it is, what's going on?"

"Ah good question Peter, good question. I've got Crysta."

St Peter had known about his Guv trying to get Crysta ever since the cherub had failed to bring her up here all those years ago. The Devil was refusing to hand her over and God had been trying to find a way ever since to take her back.

Too much time on their hands, St Peter thought, but replied, "Really and how's that then?"

"She killed that Deer." God answered with excitement in his voice.

"Ok I'm missing something, how is that a good thing to be happy about?" St Peter at this point was thinking that his Guv had finally gone tonto.

"No, she took its life to take away its misery. That's a deed worthy of someone to come to Heaven for. If she were a bad person she would have left it to suffer. That pointy bearded idiot can't talk himself out of this one. Crysta will finally be where she should have been all along."

"Ok, but what if she doesn't want to come here. I mean he lets her still roam around the world and be with her family and friends." St Peter enquired slightly warily.

"He has her soul Peter, how can she possibly like that. I'll make her whole again. How could she not want that?" God retorted.

"She'll have to leave Earth though, the people she loves." St Peter continued, realising though that he may be pushing his luck.

"I'll give her peace and ease. She has been without her soul so long now she has learnt to drown that feeling that something is missing. It's the piece of her that makes her who she is. What she is now is a shell. She knew today while she was knelt with that deer that she should feel something but she can't. Imagine if it was a member of her family or a friend. You know that's not right Peter."

"Yes Guv I know what you are saying. She may not have her soul but she is still around her family and friends." St Peter felt exasperated that the Guv was missing the point he was trying to get across.

"Ok Peter for you I'll give her the choice when it comes to it. I'm going to get together and have a chat with him downstairs first. The ball is finally in my court." God gave St Peter a mischievous grin.

St Peter just shook his head and sighed.

CHAPTER SEVEN

They met somewhere neutral, Switzerland. They were sat on top of a mountain peak. Even though it was summer below, the cap still had a little snow. God looked around admiring his handiwork. The beautiful surroundings, the blue sky, how the little bit of snow peppered the landscape with the Sun beaming down on them and a few wispy clouds below. The Devil however looked around with bored disdain.

"Well I got your e-mail, this must be important to want to meet. What do you want then Beardy?"

"I want Crysta." God boomed

"Yes I know you do and do you have to boom like that? If there had been more snow up here you could have started an avalanche and for once a natural disaster would really be your fault and not blamed on me."

"Humph, well of course." God said in a much quieter voice and clearing his throat with slight embarrassment. "Crysta took the life of a Deer to take away its pain. This proves without any doubt that she should in fact be up in Heaven with me." God finished with relish and finality in his voice.

"Oh really is that so." the Devil replied lighting up a very expensive Cuban cigar. "Ok, so if I did in fact hand Crysta over to you, as you have put forward such a strong argument. Then what do I get in return?"

This wasn't exactly what God had expected and he paused in thought. "Well, I have a cherub I'm very upset with right now. You can have him, be your secretary or something."

"Oh dear Beardy you really haven't thought this through at all have you?" the Devil smugly replied

"Look just give her to us and stop calling me Beardy." God replied with exasperation in his voice.

"How can I not? It dominates most of your face. I can't believe after all these years you still look exactly the same. The long white hair, beard, the dress and those open toed sandals that your son made a little enterprise out of inventing I hear."

"Well I'm a traditionalist, I don't need to pretend to be flash like you. People expect certain things when they come up to me."

"I'm sure people expect me to look like I did in the olds days with the ole horns and pointy tail and all that nonsense. Well life is just full of disappointments so I like to continue them when they come down to me. This suits me better. The tail was a pain in the arse, literally."

"Do you have to smoke that thing? You're ruining my atmosphere?" God replied, as he didn't have anything else to come back with. "People get Cancer from those things and cigarettes thanks to you."

"Ah Cancer, that and the cold is some of my best work. I love how people still smoke even though there is a chance of dying. People aren't very bright. Then again making people crave things, find them addictive, I believe was a clever move. God I'm good."

"No you're not! You're evil, you're the Devil." snapped God

"It's just a saying; don't get your knickers in a twist, if you in fact wear any under that robe of yours. Yikes there's a horrible thought. So still haven't sorted out a cure for my cold yet? Thought you could do anything." the Devil said with sarcasm in his voice.

"There is plenty out there to help combat the worst of it. Besides we have digressed somewhat" God jumped in quickly. The cold had been a nightmare to sort out. He was annoyed that how to cure it completely was still a mystery to him after all this time. "Crysta, what are we going to do about her? She is the worst employee you have so why keep hold of her? Just to annoy me?"

"Ah Mr Beardy you have answered your own question. I'm quite fond of Crysta actually she keeps me posted at what goes on in the world. Good to keep up with these things I feel."

"Poppy cock. Crysta rarely even watches the news. Even I know that she isn't one that's up on world affairs." God was irritated by how the whole conversation had gone and realised he was no better off than he was before. "I will be in touch, Good day to you Sam." and with a flick of his robe he disappeared. The Devil looked around for a brief moment dropping his cigar onto the floor and stomping it into the grass. A hole appeared behind him with some stairs dropping down into gloominess. The Devil turned around and sauntered down them. The hole closed itself leaving no mark to show it was ever there.

CHAPTER EIGHT

Crysta was on what is known in the Army as a Naafi break. Traditionally it starts at 10am and you were given half an hour. This was so people could go to the Naafi shop to get a mid morning snack to see them through until lunch break at 12.30pm. That's the problem with the Army, your eating patterns are totally dictated to you. Evening scoff was normally about 1730hrs, which is way too early because guaranteed you are hungry again by 2030hrs. Takeaway places willing to deliver, or are nearby, tend do very well because of this.

Cookhouse food is generally rubbish. The Army had handed more and more over to civilian contractors and the young kids that worked for them that are supposed to be Chefs. It's laughable. The vegetarian option was 'don't eat the meat'. You only ever got one choice of meat so if it happened to be one you didn't like then you pretty much were stuck with what was left. Which were normally chips, beans and a type of veg. You were lucky if any of it was cooked properly.

Food and accommodation automatically came out of your wages and majority of the time people were going out and buying their own food as well. This annoyed almost everyone. It was only really breakfast Crysta went to as it's hard to ruin cereal. Crysta and the other girl on her floor had bought a tabletop hob and a fridge so they could make themselves what they wanted. Mostly they got take out, but at least they had a choice to eat what they wanted when they wanted.

So Crysta was on her Naafi break. The shop was quite small and it was always packed at these times. You had a sit down area next door that had comfy chairs, a pool table and a TV. The bar was also there, but the grid was across the front. It didn't open until 2000hrs. Through another door was a cafe that sold pretty decent food. You could get meals like pie, mash and beans, or spag bol. Sandwiches made to order or baguettes. The ones ready made up already went quick. It was a Godsend. (Actually he had nothing to do with it but it's just another one of those sayings). Majority of people went to the Rendezvous instead of the cookhouse for lunch. Some people tried not to out of principal that they had already paid for a meal, so they were going to eat it. Well try too anyway. When it was the end of the month most people had to eat in the cookhouse because they were normally skint by then. You always had a room over your head and food (plausible) even if you didn't have a penny to your name. With every down there is an up I suppose. The Army life has to have some plus points otherwise no one would join.

Crysta was sat with Smudge (surname Smith), John boy (surname Walton, which was why he got called John Boy from the TV show The Waltons. It wasn't his real name), Geordie (because he was from Newcastle. Real name Crysta couldn't remember. People from Birmingham were called Brummy. Scousers were obviously from Liverpool and were always getting told to ay ay ay calm down. The people, who took the mickey out of them by saying that, found it wouldn't be long before they would have to ask for their wallet back. Manchester were Mancs. Hardly anyone got called by their real name. The list is endless. It would either be because of where they came from or somehow worked out by your surname or how you looked. For example one of Crysta's friends is called Lurch. This is because he is tall and a bit slow. He walks slightly bent over which gave him the impression he had a hump of some sort. Genuinely a really nice guy, but not the brightest of sparks. Crysta was just Crissy, Chris, Sloany or pepperoni because it rhymed with Sloany. Being called Pepperoni was quite ironic, as Crysta didn't eat any red meat at all, or Pork. Turkey and Chicken were fine because she didn't find them cute. Crysta didn't find fish attractive either but didn't like the taste of most of them. A fish finger and ketchup buttie, a favourite in the block, just didn't work for her. A pot noodle sarnie however went down a treat. She could cope with tuna sandwiches mixed with loads of salad cream but that was about it. Maybe a Tuna steak, but only if it had a salsa of some sort, or was covered in batter.

One of Crysta's good mates and sort of boyfriend is a guy nicknamed Tumble. His full name is Sebastian Dwyer. During basic training one of the instructors said his surname sounded like Dryer so they started calling him Tumble. It has stuck ever since. The first date they went on was to watch the Liverpool v's Man Utd match. Well it wasn't a proper date. Half the block came with them, so it was really a night out on the drink. Crysta followed Liverpool and Tumble Manc. None Man U supporters called them by another name that rhymed with Manc. As the date wasn't quite intimate they decided that whoever's team lost, that person would have to buy the other one a meal. As it worked out Liverpool lost through some rubbish refereeing that allowed Man U to be given an unfair penalty. This left the score at 2 – 1. When it came to the meal though Tumble still paid as he was trying to impress Crysta. Crysta however, not trying to impress him at all, got drunk on the wine she let him buy and walked into the glass doors of the block when she took herself off to bed. Not a great start but it was early days.

Crysta wasn't sure if it would ever be more than just the occasional snog because he was almost like a brother to her. They were always bickering and ribbing each other but it was flirty as well, so maybe. He wasn't the sort of guy Crysta would ideally like to go out with. Well Crysta thought Will Smith was gorgeous so Seb was the wrong colour for a start. Seb was 34 and taller than Crysta but not too tall. Crysta not only disliked small guys but also couldn't bare the thought of hugging a tall guy and staring at his belly button. When Seb hugged Crysta she could nestle nicely into his chest and feel his arms around her. He wasn't defined but he was stocky and played football that kept him in semi decent shape. He kept his hair Army regulation short and was balding a little on top. He blamed the Army beret for this. He claimed the many years of taking it on and off had rubbed his hair follicles away to the point that they would never grow back. He wore glasses and worst of all, he was ginger. Thankfully his hair was short and grey enough for it not to be blatantly obvious so Crysta could live with it. The main thing was he made her laugh and they got on great.

"I hear you upset an RAF officer today Crysta because you asked what rank he was." Tumble asked teasingly. He had just come over from watching the footie results on the TV.

"Yeah. Well, I don't understand all those blue and black lines. They look like bar codes. When I asked him he tapped his rank tabs like that was going to help." Crysta replied defensively.

"Apparently the more lines the higher the rank." Geordie pointed out knowingly

"Really!" Crysta said sarcastically "Well one, you would have to know how many lines meant whatever rank, and two, even if I did know that, what was I supposed to do? Ask him to bend down so I could count the lines on his shoulders. You're an idiot Geordie."

"Well ay, I was just saying mind, don't be getting yourself into a tizzy"

"I don't get the Navy either. It's all gold lines and swirly stuff. It looks a bit gay if you ask me" John boy interjected before Crysta could retort back.

"I'm pretty sure ours is really confusing to them as well. I mean sometimes when it comes to Army officers even I have to double check. I mean they're all just sir and maam to us aren't they? Who cares whether they're Flt commanders or whatever?" Crysta continued.

"Yeah, you're right. You have to salute them regardless of whether you know what rank they are." Tumble agreed.

"I hate saluting. I always try to be carrying something in both hands so I don't have to." Lurch suddenly added to the conversation after being previously caught up with eating his crisps.

This got met with silence. Most of what Lurch said was random and could generally stop a conversation dead.

"Okay, anyway. It's twenty- five past guys, time to get back to work." pointed out Crysta

"Hey, who died and made you boss?" Seb asked cheekily

"Me my dear." Crysta replied, taking the advantage of the fact that he was just about to get to his feet and shoving him back into the chair "Besides I am a higher rank than you."

"Don't I know it. Don't let the power go to your head now, you'll not get your big head out the door."

"Whatever Seb, come on dinkus, let's go"

Lurch followed behind with a can of coke in both hands just in case they bumped into an officer on the way back to work.

I would just like to point out that it is common for people to talk to each other this way with insults and stuff. The more they do it generally the closer as mates they are. Obviously people you didn't like were also called offensive names; the difference was you actually meant it.

CHAPTER NINE

Jesus was chilling out in his pad. He was wearing a sarong and of course the sandals that took his name. He designed them because he liked air to his feet. Why people ever thought to wear them with socks he had no idea. It looked ridiculous. It had his woodwork workshop at one end. The workshop was where he started his sandal outlet. His idea not only took off in heaven but also had made it to earth. Arch Angel Gabrielle nicked his design and patented it. He never returned back to work. He was a millionaire living in Los Angeles now. He thought the name sounded like lost Angel and felt a kinship with it. He was going under the name Gabe, and is apparently, as Jesus found out from his website, really big on the gay scene.

Jesus was into woodwork, a skill he had learnt from Joseph his dad. Yes his dad and Mary was his mum. God had approached Mary when she was pregnant and told him that she was going to give birth to a special boy. He was to be a prophet that was to go out in his name and preach. Jesus was supposed to teach the Jews to chill out a bit on the strict followings of their religion and lighten up. Too many animals were getting needlessly slaughtered and God wasn't a big fan of all that. It smacked too much of the sort of thing that devil worshippers did.

As it worked out Jesus got a bit too big for his boots and ended up starting a whole new religion and telling people he was the Son of God. That was not part of the plan. When he promised his people that he would be resurrected after he died, God took the opportunity to take control of the situation. Jesus hadn't been allowed back to Earth ever since. The only reason he hadn't been banished was because Christianity seemed to be working out ok and had many followers. Also God felt bad about the whole nails through the hands, hanging from a cross, whipping and thorns on the head bit. God had left the whole, is he, isn't he, question unanswered. I mean some people have made a living out of speculating the truth.

Jesus had kept all the stuff he had made. He had started with a pencil case. It was supposed to have a slide top but he couldn't make it work. It was, in the end, just a rectangle box with an open top with JC carved in the side. He had obviously progressed since. He'd had a lot of time to improve. He had just completed Noah's Ark with all the animals going in two by two.

At the other end he has a double sleigh style bed with a Tempura mattress. It said on the label that it would make you feel like you were sleeping in Heaven. He was willing to see how close this advertising claim was. Well he did know for real what that was like. He had to admit it was pretty damn good. He took his interior design straight out of the IKEA catalogue. The room was full of Swedish flat pack furniture. Stood on an oak computer desk with one drawer were 3 19inc screen monitors. One of them bleeped an incoming message alarm. Jesus came over to the screen where he had been lounging and listening to his new top of the range IPOD.

Great, he thought after he had opened the message. The boss wants to see me. This can't be good.

He donned his Dolce and Gabbana shades and walked over to the lift. As he stood waiting he admired himself in the mirror. He no longer had the beard, it made him look old. His hair was shoulder length but currently tied back. He had seen premiership footballers with this look. It was fashionable. All the people that said he looked like a girl were just fuddy duddies that didn't know what was IN. Stuck in their ways, I mean they all still wear the clothes from the era they died in. What is that all about? Move on with the times already. With this final thought the lift pinged and he got in and settled himself down for the long boring journey.

"Ah Jesus you got my e-mail then?" God said looking up as Jesus walked in.

"Yes Guv. What seems to be the problem?"

"I need you to go to Earth to join the Army. You'll be a Chef at the camp where Crysta works. I want you to watch her and if possible kidnap her," God said not fully looking Jesus in the eye. He realised the implications of what he was asking him to do.

"Say what now?" Jesus asked "You want me to do what now? Join the bloody Army and kidnap some girl. Have you gone completely nuts?" a slightly confused and exasperated Jesus enquired.

"Now listen here. First don't swear at me."

"I never" Jesus interrupted "Bloody is in your good book. There's a poem about it. Goes something like, Bloody in the Bible.."

"Yes, Yes." God cut in "I'm fully aware of the ditty and you know full well that it isn't used in that context. Also to answer your question, no I'm not nuts. Crysta has proved she belongs here and still that idiot downstairs won't give her up. I've had enough of playing games. Go down and get her."

"Well for one. It will stand out a mile that I'm no trained soldier so that cover story will get blown straight away. Also a chef I ain't. I mean yeah of course I can do the whole turn water into wine and bread and fish. That's it though. The whole of my repertoire, and last time I checked kidnapping wasn't on there either."

"Jesus I think you forget who you are talking too. I won't send you down there without all the skills you need. When you arrive you will be surprised how much you are capable off. You'll fit in just fine. That stupid ponytail will have to go of course. Soldiers do not have long hair."

"What? But it's the fashion. This is completely unfair. Send me down as a civilian Chef that way I can keep my hair." a slightly panicked Jesus replied.

"No Jesus this is the way it's going to go. Now report to me in a week I'm sending you down then. Probably a good idea to watch relevant DVD's in the meantime to get some background on what to expect. Thank you goodbye." God said with finality in his voice. Jesus stood there for a moment with his mouth going up and down but no sound coming out. It was no use. Whatever he said wouldn't help his case. So I'm going back to Earth after all this time, was what come to mind initially. With a bit more thought he decided that this might not be a bad thing. Maybe I can pay Gabe a visit while I'm down there. I owe him a punch in the mouth for getting rich off my design the…..A very unchristian word came into his mind. He shook his head. He looked up at the boss. He was pretending to be busy on his PC. Jesus turned around and made his way back to the lift.

When he got back to his room much later on, he went straight to his PC and went onto 'Ask Jeeves'. He typed in. British Army Chefs. What do I need to know about becoming one? Even this was a bit too much for Jeeves to be able to answer properly.

CHAPTER TEN

Crysta was sat in her bunk in the block. It had room for a double bed. It had a couple of overhead cupboards and a double wardrobe next to it. 3 fixed shelves were on the wall opposite. Crysta had her telly on the bottom one and 4 ceramic decorative plates on stands on the top one. They had pictures of horses on them. Crysta loved animals but horses were her favourite. Crysta did the whole pony club thing when she was a kid. She had never been able to get a horse of her own though. The family moved around too much with her Dad being military. Crysta hadn't done horse riding for a long time, especially since she joined the Army. It is more expensive than it used to be. She enquired at local stables once and it was £15 for forty five minutes. Crysta refused to pay that much when you weren't even getting a full hour.

Crysta loved horses so much in fact she had a tattoo of one on her shoulder. A couple of mates and her after a day on the beach decided they would go off and get one. Being slightly sunburnt this probably wasn't the smartest move in the world. They all piled in the nearest tattoo parlour they came across. Her friends had got sensible little ones with flowers and hearts and things. Crysta however wanted a black stallion rearing up. The tattoo artist said that with it being mainly black you would lose a lot of the detail. Crysta settled for a horse galloping that was of various bright colours. Her friends said it was a bit big (it took up her whole shoulder blade) and the colours made it look a little like a My little pony. Crysta's parents weren't too thrilled when she told them. They didn't berate her for it though. She was in the Army now and was old enough to do what she wanted, with or without their approval. Crysta thought it was worth the bleeding, pain and money however, and that's what counts. A couple of years later Crysta had got a tattoo on her right ankle of a little devil with a pitch fork. It had the words Bad girl scrolled underneath. It was her private joke.

The middle shelf had bits and bobs: - Soft toys, framed photos of friends, family and Prince. She also had a notice board to the left of the shelves that were covered in photos. They were mostly she had to acknowledge, pictures of her out drinking with mates. There was a sink that was right next to the door. It had a shelf above for your toothbrush/paste etc and a mirror. It was compact but it was home.

If you went out of Crysta's room there was another bunk opposite hers. Looking left was a four-man room that was currently empty. The unit she was in at the moment had a larger ratio of men to women. Going right took you to the bathroom. It had three toilet stalls, one shower, one bath with an additional door. This gave you the chance to get some privacy. A hard thing to do in a block. Especially as someone could just stand on the toilet, and look over the top at you in the bath. You also had another three sinks lined up across the wall opposite the toilets. They all had a mirror above them. Opposite, a small kitchen/drying room. It had an industrial washing machine that was so old fashioned you had to lift the lid before the spin to add the softener. If you didn't put the powder in the bottom first and just pour it on top of your clothes. The end result was clean (ish) clothes but with white powder streaks that hadn't washed out properly. This is something you learn v quickly to get right. The army also charged you a quid to use it, the thieves.

Crysta was sat on her bed chatting to her mum when Seb walked in. Blokes weren't really allowed in the block but nobody paid much attention to the fact. Alcohol wasn't either and that rule got broke on a regular basis. The general thought behind this ban was that it was rubbish. An eighteen year old kid who had just got married was not only just about the legal age to drink, he could, and the Army couldn't touch him if he did. They even provided him with a house to drink in. So the guys who lived in the block couldn't drink in their own rooms. Yeah ok, like that wasn't going to happen.

As he walked in and went to say something Crysta quickly put her finger on her lips as the universal sign for be quiet.

"Ok Mum, thanks for letting me know. Are you going to be ok? Yeah I will be, just probably in shock. Have you told Sky. Do you want me too? No ok, well love to you and dad. I'm happy to put money towards his cremation or whatever." With hearing the word cremation Seb instantly raised an enquiring eyebrow and sat next to Crysta on the bed. He had a slightly concerned look, realising there must have been some death in the family.

"Ok, well the offer is there. He's going in the garden under the tree he liked to pee on. Ok makes sense." Confusion crossed over Seb's face for a moment and then realisation kicked in. Prince had obviously died.

"I'll try and get home soon then Mum to pay my respects, don't cry Mum you'll set me off. Going to go now. Ok love you too, Bye Mum. Yes I'm sure I'll be ok Seb is here. Ok Mum bye then, yes you too, Bye." Crysta slid her mobile shut to end the call.

"Wow that sucks. I loved him." Crysta said slightly to herself and to Seb.

"Hey if you wanna cry I won't take the mickey you know. I know how mad about animals and stuff you are."

"Nah I'm ok. It'll probably hit me later. Don't think it's sunk in yet." Crysta knew full well that she hadn't felt or cried about anything since she had lost her soul. She couldn't tell Seb that. Oh don't worry about me I have no soul, hadn't you noticed? I'm a cold hearted bitch. That's what she felt like sometimes. When her nana had died a few years back she didn't really feel anything. She used the delayed reaction that time as well. It should have made her feel awful. Seb had read her quiet pondering as a possible moment that she may actually cry. Which he didn't really want her too. He and most blokes in general, just can't cope with women when they cry. So to possible head off what he thought was going to be Crysta breaking down into tears and snot he quickly suggested that they went into town.

"Come on mate, chuck on your jeans and we'll go have a drink for poor old Prince. What did he die off anyway? Was it just old age?"

"Hmm" Seb's voice brought Crysta out of her reverie. "What? Drinks yeah sure." She jumped off her bed and went to her wardrobe. They had a comfortable enough friendship that getting dressed in front of him wasn't an issue. He'd seen her in a swimsuit. To Crysta that was being exposed as if you were naked. "His hips had gone. Classic German Shepherd problem. Sucks the poor ole boy." With her jeans dragged on and a more suitable top pulled over her head, she gave Seb a weak smile and said.

"Come on then pal let's get minging. Your round first."

"What? So your dog dies and I have to buy you a drink. My hamster died ages ago I don't remember you getting me a drink?"

"That's not the same and you know it." Crysta didn't take offence to this; she knew that it was Sebs feeble attempt to cheer her up.

"Come on stingy lets go and get your wallet." They walked out the door and down the corridor.

"What did you come and see me about anyway?" Crysta asked while they walked down the stairs.

"Oh that. Apparently an Army Chef is getting posted in."

"Really! Brill. Decent food at last. Thank God for that."

Crysta had no idea how true that statement was.

CHAPTER ELEVEN

The Devil didn't have the greatest relationship with his son. His son Damien should have been a chip off the old block. Smooth persuasive personality, with a sharp dress sense. A keenness to get on in the business. Someone who would eventually take over to give Sam the chance to retire. His retirement was going to many more decades off yet. Damien was nothing like the son of the Devil should be. He was a rocker. He had long curly hair that covered most of his face. He idolised Slash. He tried to dress and act like him. He had the top hat and everything. Slash was a guy who used to play in a group called Guns 'n' Roses. When the group split up it was the saddest day of his life.

Damien knew that when one of his dad's lawyer like cronies came into the middle of his jamming session with his band. That it couldn't be good news. His band was not very imaginably called Guns 'n' War. He decided not to keep the Roses bit. He always thought a flower was a bit poncy. He only ever saw his Dad when absolutely necessary. He avoided being with him because he was sick of the constant nagging to change his ways. His Dad's voice rang in his head "Get more involved in the business. Taking Souls is serious and one day he'd have to learn the ropes". So on and so forth, blah blah, blah. All Damien wanted to do was smoke, jam, drink and have a good time with the ladies. Just like Slash.

Damien walked into his Dad's plush office wearing his skinny leg jeans, a black T-shirt with his bands slogan on it and of course the black very worn looking, Top hat. He sat himself in the chair opposite his Dad's pulled a cigarette out of his tight jean pocket and lit it with his thumb. You don't need to own a lighter when you're the son of the Devil.

"Hey Pop" he said while swinging a leg up on to the desk.

Sam turned around from watering the new Venus flytrap he had just put into his office.

"Aaah Damien, take your feet off my desk there's a good boy."

"I ain't no dog Dad so don't talk to me like one."

Sam gave his son a steady stare. Damien took his foot off the desk. He didn't like how the black pupils just stared through him without blinking. His own father freaked him out. Damien himself had the trademark black pupils. He had never tried to stare himself out though so they didn't freak him.

"Damien, I can hardly see your face with all that hair. When I look at you all I see is lots of hair with a nose stuck out of it. Oh and of course there is that hat. Does it come off? I imagine you probably sleep with it on" Sam walked around his chair and sat down opposite Damien.

"This hat used to belong to Slash himself. I managed to nick it after I went up to watch one of their concerts years ago. People would offer me thousands for this on e-bay."

Sam leaned forward on the desk and tried to see his son properly through all the hair. He leaned back again giving up.

"Interesting story Damien." his tone though conveying that in fact it really wasn't "Now to get right down to why I asked you here. I have a job for you up top"

"What? Hell no. Dad." his voice taking on a slight whiney tone "I'm in the middle of recording an album. I can't leave now. I'm the lead guitarist"

"Damien, son." Sam paused. How did his son get like this? "I don't care about your band. You are the heir to this realm and you will pull your weight. I need you to go up top and keep and eye on a girl called Crysta." he quickly continued before his son decided he was going to carry on moaning. "I think Beardy is up to something and I want you to be around in case he is trying to pull something."

Damien wasn't expecting his Dad to say something like that. It took him back slightly. He sat there silently for a moment. He lit another cigarette and pushed the chair onto its back legs in quiet contemplation. Eventually under the cool stare of his Dad he asked

"This Crysta. She is obviously one of yours so why would Beardy want her. If she works for you she can't be an Angel now can she? What's the story then Pop?"

"I'll give you the file it's too long winded. Now you're going up as a private in the Army to her unit. I'm afraid that mass of hedge you have on your head will need to be chopped off."

Damien really hadn't expected that. His mouth gaped open and the cigarette fell into his lap. The near burning of his precious jewels took his attention away for a moment but not for long enough. He managed to get all four legs of the chair back on the floor before falling backwards.

"You want me to do what? I'm not cutting my hair off man. No frigging way." he was angry and panicking at the same time.

"Now son I know how fond of your um, yes hair, if you can call it that. You don't and won't have a choice. I'll be sending you up in a couple of days so go and get your stuff together." his voice had an edge of annoyance to it

"I don't know anything about the Army. Come on Dad this is mental you know it is." he was worried. He knew he wasn't going to win but hoping a last ditch effort would change his Dad's mind. His Dad merely rested his elbows on the desk and put his fingertips together and stared. Defeated Damien started to walk out of the office.

"You'll be ready in a couple of days. I'll make sure you know everything you need to know about the Army so don't worry. Now go and get your hair cut."

Damien paused with his hand on the doorknob. He was going to turn round and have the last sarcastic word. He didn't know what to say so he just stepped out sheepishly. He took some of his hair in his hand and looked at it. It was like a comfort blanket. He hated his Dad for doing this. Don't worry, easy for him to say. I hope this Crysta is good looking, or at least pretty, he thought, it may make it worth my while.

CHAPTER TWELVE

Crysta was sat in the cookhouse with the usual crew. Geordie was on leave but everyone else was sat down at the long trestle table. Crysta was sat next to Seb. Opposite was John boy and Smudge next to him and over at the hot plate trying to decide whether he wanted to have the chicken curry or fish pie was Lurch. The new chef had definitely made an impact to the quality of the food and the fact he now had a choice was a thought process that Lurch was struggling with. He went with the chicken curry with chips and came across to the table. He placed his tray down and walked over to get his cutlery and some squash from the drinks dispenser. Both the drinks coolers had a different choice of squash. Before it was blackcurrant or orange and the other one always only ever had water in it. Today one had the blackcurrant and the other orange. Scared that he may not get the chance to have one of each again he filled a cup of each. The cutlery then had to be put in his mouth to allow him to carry both cups back to the table.

"hmwot abboo m choime dem?" he asked everyone as he approached the table.

"Wot? I'm not a dentist Lurch I can't understand you with your mouth full." Crysta pointed out.

"Wot about the choice then?" Lurch repeated now sat down with the knife and fork removed from his mouth. The napkin they were wrapped in looked a bit soggy.

"Yeah making quite a few changes this new guy ain't he. I'm impressed." John boy said shovelling curry and some fish pie into his mouth.

"How come you got to have curry and the fish pie?" Lurch asked

"New boy didn't stop me. Don't think he knows we're only supposed to get one choice. Don't taste too great together. Separately nice, but together, not a good combination."

"Why did you get both then? That's gross by the way." Crysta said screwing her face up to back up her statement.

"Well it all comes out the same don't it." was John Boy's reply

"Nice topic at the dinner table this is." Seb interjected "Do we even know what his name is?"

"Who's?" The question came from Lurch

"The new chef idiot."

The table went quiet for a moment. "That'll be a no then."

"I'll go ask him." Crysta volunteered. With that she slid the plastic black chair back and went over to the hot plate.

"Hi" she said as she approached him.

He was stood in a white apron and hat and looked very unsure of himself. Jesus was missing his ponytail. He'd moved in the four-man bunk a couple of days ago and was trying to adapt. It was all a bit bizarre. Being back on Earth was taking a bit of getting used to. He knew how it had moved on. He'd watch the changes from afar. Being down here among it almost made him feel agoraphobic. He kept thinking he was going to have a panic attack. He was shocked at how good at cooking the Guv had made him. He didn't have to think. It was like his body had a will of its own. He'd be there chopping, slicing and making amazing meals but at the end of it all he had no idea really of how he just did it. It's a bit like when you're driving and you're tired. You don't actually fall asleep but you can't remember driving down that last stretch of road. You must have done because you're just about to pull into work. The journey itself though is a bit of a blur.

He was struggling with the slang words. The Army had a language of their own it seemed. The Guv had supplied him with a book to look up the main ones. He also knew that the woman walking towards him was her. Crysta. The one he'd been sent down here for. He'd seen her a couple of times but didn't know quite what to say to her. It's not like he could stroll up to her. Chuck her over his shoulder and just take her up to heaven. How in God's name was he going to do this? In his head he was thinking, No don't come over, don't come over. Great she's come over.

"Hey." he replied and gave her a sheepish smile. Crysta waited to see if he was going to add anything else. He was just there looking at her with what Crysta thought looked like panic in his eyes. 'Ok' she thought 'Obviously a bit shy and not very talkative.' She was about to walk away but then she remembered why she'd gone over in the first place.

"Your food is a hell of an improvement on the stuff we used to have" Jesus winced slightly at the use of the word hell and nodded with a quick "yeah, thanks."

"Do you have a name then saviour of the cookhouse food?"

For a split second because Crysta called him saviour he thought 'She knows who I am. She knew all along and the Guv has sent me down here on a big wind up. No she can't, calm down. If this does work out to be some big joke though I won't be impressed.

"So do you have a name or not?" Crysta asked again butting in on his thoughts.

"Yeah sure it's Jeeee." He stopped there. His brain kicking in on time to stop him blurting out that his name was Jesus.

"Do you have enough eee's in that?" Crysta asked

"Sorry, no, Gee. Please call me Gee."

"Ok Gee it is. Is there a surname with that?"

Oh God, the now newly named Gee thought. What can my surname be?

"It's um Gee." he paused "It's um Gee Christian." he finally blurted out.

"Oh Kay Mr um Gee Christian it was nice to meet you. I'll see you around no doubt. Keep up the good work with the food." Crysta walked back over to the table where Seb had been watching the whole exchange out of the corner of his eye.

"He's a bit strange that one" Crysta said sitting down again "He may be able to cook but he was struggling to tell me his name back there. He's like a nervous rabbit caught in the head lights or something."

"So after all that, what is his name." Seb enquired

"Gee, Gee Christian. Apparently. Dunno, there's somet not right about him."

"I've seen the stuff he's got in his room" Smudge added to the conversation. All eyes turned to him.

"He's in the four man room off my bunk" Each block had four floors and each floor had two contained areas set out like Crysta's. One four-man room at the end, the two bunks and the kitchen opposite the bathroom as you walked through a door into the corridor. Across the landing it was the same. Smudge had been the only one on his side in the bunk for a few months now and had gotten used to his own space. He had been slightly put out when the new boy had been moved in but so far he had been quiet and kept to himself. Smudge had hardly noticed he was there.

"I forgot he'd moved in by you." Seb said

"I'm guessing he's not a great conversationalist." added Crysta.

"You said somet about his stuff. What about his stuff?" John Boy asked not letting the conversation go off on a tangent.

"He's got some right guchi stuff guys I'm telling ya. Flat screen TV. The new Apple laptop. He's got one of those mattresses that mould to your body shape. It's well comfy. He's even got one of those Wii things. It's like bloody heaven in there."

"One" Seb said "Why were you lying on his mattress? And two. His parents must be loaded or somet coz there is no way his private wage could cover that lot."

Just before Smudge got the chance to say that he only sat on the end of his bed while he tried to say Hi and just have a chat with the new bloke. Which he thought was like pulling teeth. He had a look around. Told him his name and when it didn't look like the conversation was going anywhere he'd left. He'd left thinking 'Man, he's got some nice gear'. But before he could say all that Crysta said

"Oh poor little rich boy. No wonder he seems so lost. He probably got forced into this by his parents or somet."

"Don't Oh him Crissy, he's a bit of a nancy boy actually when you look at him." This was Seb's snap judgement of the guy.

"Nah, he's nice. Just a bit shy and a lot out of his depth. We'll ask him if he wants to come to the Naafi tonight."

"Look I'm sure he'll be fine in his room with all his gadgets. Probably won't want to hang with common people like us."

"Seb give the guy a break you don't even know him. If you are nice to him he may let you play Golf on his Wii. Smudge when you get back later on ask him over to the bar ok." Crysta took on her being a bossy woman tone.

"Yeah fine, whatever." Smudge answered. Crysta looked at Seb waiting for him to start an argument.

"Wot? Yeah fine. I don't care. I'm sure he's a nice guy. Probably doesn't have the Golf game for the Wii though. Doesn't look the type to play sports. Probably have all the girly games."

Crysta just sighed and stood up. They all followed suit and took their trays over to the clearing rack.

"John Boy!" Seb gasped "Have you just dropped your arse, coz that stinks."

"I can't help it must be the fish pie combo I ate."

"You stink mate, smells like somet has crawled up your arse and died."

"You need pulling through with a Christmas tree or somet mate, that's not good." Crysta added with her hand over her nose. "At least we are going out into the fresh air." They all grabbed their berets off the hooks by the door and nearly ran out of the door with Seb shouting "Gas, Gas, Gas, get your respirator on people or you could die."

Am I really on Earth or has the Guv sent me to Hell and I can't tell the difference, Jesus mused, this is an absolute nightmare. I need to get this done and get back ASAP. He paused; I just used an Army abbreviation. Right God what's happening to me, he stormed mentally giving a quick accusing look heavenward. You are definitely getting e-mail from me tonight. Then he pondered to himself, I don't see how I can pull this off, as he looked back down to the floor despairingly with a shaking of his head.

CHAPTER THIRTEEN

Crysta had her towel wrapped round her and was walking down the corridor to get a shower when it happened.

"Oh Shit!"

"Ah Crysta so nice of you to join us, so glad you dressed for the occasion." the Devil said. He was seated behind his desk with a smirk on his face.

"I'm glad you find this amusing. Can't you check first before you drag me here?"

"I would apologise but I wouldn't mean it. Take a seat I would like to introduce you to somebody."

Other than the lawyer that came to Crysta on the day she got hit by the car, Crysta had never met anyone else in Hell other than the Boss. Crysta looked around and saw stood in the corner a very good-looking guy. He was about 5ft 8, slight but toned, almost athletic looking. He was wearing a Prada suit. Black. His hair was almost jet black. It was layered at the back but had a fringe that fell across his forehead at a slant. He had the deepest blackest eyes. Crysta guessed straight away from the eyes who he was.

"You must be Damien." Crysta stated, addressing him.

"How did you know my name?"

"Lucky guess." In her head she was thinking 'who would have thought the Devil's son would be so good looking. I'm sat here in a towel as well, looking far from lush. Great, just dandy that is' she dragged her eyes away from Damien to look at his Dad. Weird thinking of the Boss as a Dad. I mean who is the mother?

"Okay so I've met your son. Still can't see the emergency that got you to bring me here with only a towel on."

"He's going to be going back with you. I know beardy is going to try something but I don't know what. Damien here is going to earn his keep for a change and keep an eye on things."

"Beardy. Keep an eye on things. What in the Hell are you talking about? He can't just show up with me. You'll have to sort him out a room. Pretend he's a soldier or something. I can't stash him away in my bunk you know. It doesn't have any hiding places and there is barely enough room for me. I'm pretty sure he'll be noticed when it comes to block inspections."

"Have you quite finished miss Sloane?"

Crysta paused and took a breath. "Yeah but"

"No buts' Crysta." the Devil cut in "you forget who you are talking to. Don't you think I have made arrangements? To make things easier I'll send him up tomorrow. When he shows up I want you to make out like your old friends. I wanted to make sure you met beforehand so you knew who he was."

"Why do things need an eye on them? I don't understand what is going on." a very confused Crysta pointed out.

"Damien will let you know the details tomorrow. I'm sure you'll be great friends."

Crysta looked at Damien who was looking at the floor. He had been up the top quite a few times for concerts and stuff. He wasn't thrilled with his new look and even less thrilled at pretending to be a soldier. It may be every young boys dream but it wasn't his. He wanted to stay with his band. He still didn't fully comprehend what his Dad wanted from him. Just keep an eye on Crysta he said. He thinks God is going to make a move sometime soon. He didn't care about any of it and now he was stuck watching some Army chick. Fan bloody tastic. Ok she wasn't ugly or anything.

"I'll be seeing you tomorrow then" he said with a slightly sulky tone.

Then she was back in the corridor with a dimming image of her Boss with a very smug smile on his face.

"Crysta I can't believe you haven't even had a shower yet. What the Hell have you been doing all this time?" it was Seb. He had just walked into the corridor just as she got back. Crysta found it ironic that he had asked what in the Hell she had been doing.

"I've been on the phone. I won't be long. You go down the bar I'll meet you there."

"Ok no worries. You ok. You look a bit shook up. Nothing else has died has it?"

"Subtle as ever Seb. No I'm good, thanks for asking but not caring."

"I do care" he replied in a jovial tone "Oh by the way we asked the new boy if he wanted to come down. He said he couldn't he had to catch up on his e-mails or somet. Smudge was right though. He does have some well guchi stuff in his room."

"Well we can't force the guy I guess. Well I need to get a shower so I'll catch up later ok."

"You sure do need a shower. Sure you don't want some company in there. I don't mind getting another shower if you're going to make it worth my while."

"Oh funny. I never get tired of those sort of comments" Crysta retorted.

"Oh well can't blame a man for trying. Hurry up the alcohol won't drink itself." and with a cheeky grin he was gone.

Crysta stood in the corridor for a second while the events of the last twenty minutes or so went through her head. She hadn't actually heard from the Boss for a while. She had kind of hoped that he had given up on her and was letting her just get on with things. No, and now he was sending his son up to keep and eye on her. She didn't know why and she had to pretend to be his friend. He was good looking though. Crysta probably wouldn't have thought that if she had seen him before when he was hiding behind all his hair. Crysta figured she would have to see what happens tomorrow and try not to stress about it today. She also thought it was only fair to see if she could persuade Gee to come to the Naafi with her, help him to get to know the lads better.

CHAPTER FOURTEEN

Jesus was sat in his bunk e-mailing the Guv .

What have you done to me, I feel like my body has been snatched by some body snatchers or something?

He pressed send…a couple of seconds later the computer beeped to indicate a reply

What an inane thing to say. What is your progress? Why didn't you say yes to going to the bar with Seb?

How did he know…oh of course he's God, all seeing and all that…

I hate it here, I'm freaking out, can I come back? Can't you get someone else down here to do this?….send…..beep.

No!

"That's it just No, well thanks for nothing." Jesus said out loud looking at the ceiling in frustration. His terminal beeped

I can hear you; I hear and see all things.

"Well then Guv, I'm not going to bother using e-mail anymore. I'll just talk to you like this then shall I? He said with annoyance in his voice. The computer beeped again.

If you wish, it is of no difference to me. Now go and gain Crysta's friendship. Once you have her trust you will be able to make your move.

"Make my move, and what move do you propose that I do Guv? I have to say I don't have the foggiest idea of what I'm going to do." There was a slightly longer pause then his incoming mail signalled.

Not my problem. You're down there so think of something. Let me know when you have made progress.

Almost fuming Jesus whispered under his breath...." thanks for nothing." then he heard the beep

I heard that..

"Good" he yelled. There was a knock on the door, which stopped him from continuing to yell up at the ceiling.

"Can I come in?"

It was Crysta. "Uh yeah I guess, come in"

"Are you Ok?" Crysta asked looking around "I thought I heard you talking to someone." She could clearly see there was no one around.

"Um I sort of was yelling at my computer. It wasn't doing what I wanted so I yelled at it. Silly really but it makes me feel better"

"I have no patience either when those things run slow. You have some guchi gear in here Gee." "Guchi? Is that a good thing? I thought that was a name in fashion?"

"Well it is. It's just...I dunno. It's just somet you say. I haven't played on one of these Wii things yet. I hear they're good"

"They're more fun when you can play with a partner or in a team. You can get quite a sweat up with them." Gee registered what he just said and blushed slightly. Luckily Crysta wasn't looking at him but was picking up and inspecting the controls.

"What's this bit then?"

"That's a nun chuck. You need that and the Wii hand control for boxing, rowing, swimming and stuff."

"Anything you need two hands for then basically. Cool. Can I have a go?"

"Sure, what do you want to have a go at first?"

"Boxing sounds good. See if I can kick your ass"

"Um, ok. You know it's on screen and not for real yes?"

Crysta gave him a long steady stare and eventually said "Yes Gee I do know that. I'm not that thick you know."

"Oh yes of course…I didn't mean…Ok let me just set it up."

I would think it was a coincidence that Crysta came to my door just then, Gee thought, but then again it probably wasn't. I have to remember whom I'm working for.

CHAPTER FIFTEEN

"Where were you last night?" Seb asked almost angrily the minute Crysta stepped out of the block.

"And a good morning to you too Seb."

"So?"

"So what?"

"Where were you? You didn't come down to the bar. I went up to your room to see what was taking you so long and you weren't there."

"Oh right. I went up to see if Gee would change his mind about coming down and we ended up playing on the Wii for most of the night. I tell you what my arm is a bit sore this morning. I'm rubbish at tennis and baseball. Not as bad as I thought I would be at Golf though. He has got sporty games and not girlie ones like you thought he would have. It's brill fun."

"Well good for you and him. You could have text me or somet to let me know what you were up to."

"What are you, my keeper?" then a flashback of what the Boss last told her appeared in her mind. "Did a new guy show up last night or this morning?"

The change of conversation threw Seb for a moment. "I'm not sure. Why do you ask? Need another new team mate to play on the Wii with?"

"Oh grow up Seb. No I got told there was a new guy coming in. You being a guy I figured you would know before me."

"Well I've not seen anyone. Who told you there was someone coming in?"

"Ah that I can't tell you. It's top secret. If I tell you then I'll have to shred you." Crysta said playfully "So are we going to breakfast then or what I'm starving."

"Sure, I said I would knock on Smudge on the way. I'm hoping your new boyfriend has done some nice scoff today. I could go a crispy bacon sarnie."

"Seb" Crysta stopped him mid walk and pulled him round so they were facing each other. "You know full well he isn't my new boyfriend. I'm just helping him settle in. He's ok. A bit shy and possibly a bit weird but ok. I heard him talking to himself last night you know."

"Really? Doesn't surprise me. He does seem a bit special, you know like special needs"

"That's cruel Seb." Crysta giggled anyway and the tension between them had gone. There is nothing like taking the mickey out of someone to regain a kinship. "I'll ask him if you can come up and have a go on the Wii tonight. You can get to know him then."

"Whatever, we'll see. Wait here I'll go and get Smudge. See if the lazy git is out of bed yet." He went through the block doors and took a left turn. "Oy Smudger you up mate?" When Seb got his bunk the door was ajar and Smudge was just getting his boots on. "Nearly, two secs. Hey I heard Crysta in the four man room with the new guy last night when I got in from the bar. Did you know about that?"

"Yeah, Crysta's outside waiting for us. She told me."

"How do feel about that? I mean I know you guys aren't like a couple or anything but you have history. I personally think he's cheeky. If buying a Wii is all it takes to get women into your room then I'm getting one."

"Smudge you would need more than a Wii to get women in here. Besides your in a bunk and don't exactly have the room."

"I wouldn't plan on playing with just the Wii if you know what I mean. I only need a bed for the sort of games I'd want to play."

"You're dreaming pal. Now hurry up and get your stuff together."

"So what about, you know, Crysta and Gee?"

"There is no Crysta and Gee ok let's get that straight. She's just helping him to settle in and stuff. She was on about another guy coming in. Do you know owt about that?"

"No but that could be him." They had reached the main doors and as they came down the stairs they could see Crysta talking to a guy who in Seb's instant opinion had a fringe that was far too long and if he was a sprog, he would use his rank on him to make sure it got cut.

"Hey Crysta ya ready?" Seb asked barely giving Damien a second glance.

"Yeah sure. Seb this is Damien. We were in basic training together. I've not seen him for ages. I didn't know you were coming to this unit." Crysta said linking arms with Damien and walking him towards the cookhouse. "Just keep walking" Crysta whispered "I can't be doing with an interrogation about you just yet."

CHAPTER SIXTEEN

When Damien and Crysta walked into the cookhouse Gee looked up and straight into Damien's black pupils. Instant recognition passed between them. Gee felt his stomach jump and Damien just gave him a mirthless smile. This, Damien considered, could be more fun than I thought.

"Morning Gee, how are you today? My arm is killing me you know."

"Yeah good Crysta cheers. I'm a bit tired though. Getting up early to prep food for you lot is hard."

"I'll bet, rather you than me mate, I so don't do mornings, especially early ones. I'll have just beans I'm gonna chuck some bread in the toaster. This is Damien by the way. I used to know him in basic."

Interesting, Jesus thought, Crysta obviously knows who he is and has a cover story for him. I'm pretty sure the Guv knows that Damien is here as well, hmmm, wonder what's going on.

"Why are you here?" Jesus blurted out loud. Meant to keep that in my head, he scorned himself.

"To have breakfast obviously." was Damien's cool reply.

Crysta watched the curious exchange from the toaster, which was taking forever. The settings were either warm bread or burnt, so you had to watch it.

"Do you guys know each other?" Crysta yelled over

"Nah" Damien replied.

Crysta was sure she saw something exchange between them. 'Nah' she thought 'there's no way anyone here on earth could know Damien, unless they were agents like me' Crysta looked at Gee. 'I wonder. He's shown up from nowhere, he knows hardly anything about the Army. The Boss has got two of them here, not good. I'm defo speaking to those two later' she felt a tap on her shoulder that made her jump, the smell of burning registered her nostrils.

"Damn it Lurch you made me jump, and my toast is frigging burnt now"

"Soz Crysta, didn't mean to."

"Lurch you should know not to speak to Crysta in the morning, especially if she hasn't eaten yet. She's a double stroppy cow."

"Yeah cheers for that Seb. Now I've got to wait another god knows how long to get some decent toast."

"Yeah well its poets day today so it can't be all bad." Smudge interjected.

"Poets day. What does that mean?" Damien queried. I hope this lot aren't a bunch of nutters like those out of that film Dead poets society. I mean that guy shot himself because his father wouldn't let him act for a living...oh purleese.

"Poets day, Piss Off Early Tomorrow is Saturday." Seb informed him.

"So are we going drinking tonight then ladies and germs or wot?" Smudge, the man who sees every weekend as an opportunity to go on the pull. His favourite chat up line was "I'm in the Army and being sent out to Afghanistan soon. I may not make it back. I could use some company tonight." It only really worked depending on how drunk the girl was, or how believable he put his story across. As he got drunker the hit rate got considerably lower.

He wasn't a bad looking lad. He was skinny, dark hair, about 5ft 9. Slightly elfish look to his ears and had no arse, as Crysta would point out. Crysta hated blokes whose waist was smaller than hers, and any guy who had longer eye lashes. Her logic being, men should have the short stubby eye lashes, like hers. Women should have long lashes. It would mean mascara had a better purpose when you put it on.

"Sure, sounds like a plan. Damien, Gee, you guys will come out won't you? Give us the chance for us all to get to know each other better." Crysta said out loud but in her head she was thinking, and give me the chance to have a word with you the pair of you.

"Yeah coz that's the caring, sharing kinda platoon we are." Seb added sarcastically.

"Shut up Seb. So guys, yay or nay?" Crysta directed her question straight at them both.

"Sure, I'm up for it. Been a while since I've been out and about." Damien said

I can't leave Crysta and him together on their own, Jesus worried so said "Sure Ok then, I'm in."

"Excellent. Let's get this day done then. Meet you all outside the block at twenty hundred hrs ok."

I hate it when they use 24hr clock, Jesus noted as he took out his little phrase book which had a time conversion clock in it as well. 8pm, right, why don't they just say that, sheesh, talk about making things unnecessarily complicated.

CHAPTER SEVENTEEN

They decided to do a pub crawl from the camp. The idea being one pint per pub. This meant two alcopops per pub for Crysta, as she could drink them quicker. Her tipple being Smirnoff ice. The red label one because it was sweeter than the black label one. She couldn't drink pints; they made her pee like a race horse. There's no fun on a night out if you have to rush to the loo every five minutes. All the guys were dressed in the usual jeans and shirt, or collared top. No blue jeans. You wouldn't be allowed in the club with original jeans. Damien had his usual rock gear on with steel toe cap boots. He wanted to wear his hat but it looked stupid with his hair short. Crysta had on her black kick flare jeans and brown fitted shirt, with her high heeled knee length boots, which would be killing her feet later. Crysta didn't do dresses or skirts, or anything remotely girly. Heels and makeup were about as good as it got.

"You look different with your hair down" Gee commented while they were stood at the bar at the fourth pub.

"Yeah well putting your hair in a bun and wearing Army uniform ain't all that flattering is it? I mean buns are so grannified."

"You look nice."

"Cheers… you must be drunk."

"No, just being truthful."

"You do know Damien don't you?"

"What makes you say that?"

"Dunno, just somet I spotted between you both in the cookhouse. Are you an agent like me?"

"I'm not sure I know what you're talking about Crysta."

"Sure you do. You work for him don't you? Don't ask me who him is either, you know full well who I mean."

"I think you have things a little confused Crysta, you've got it slightly mixed up."

"Have I? Have I really. Well would you like to make things a bit clearer for me then?" Crysta asked with anger edging into her voice.

"Look Crysta it's complicated and I'm sure you wouldn't believe me if I told you."

"Oh no. Why don't you try me?"

"Crysta you got those drinks in yet, you've been stood over here for ages" Seb interrupted.

Jesus gave out a short sigh of relief. He didn't want to go through it all with Crysta right now. Crysta gave Gee a glare then turned to Seb.

"I'm not having much luck mate, the barman is a chick, maybe you'll do better." With that she pushed the money into his hands and walked over to the toilets.

"What you been saying to upset her?"

"Nothing honest."

"Probably just time of the month or somet. Ok let's get these drinks in, see if you can grab the bar maids attention."

"Are you and Crysta a couple?"

"No, sort of, kind of. Dunno really. Why do you fancy her?" there was a touch of defensiveness in his voice.

"No, nothing like that, just asking you know. Making polite conversation."

"Right well, polite conversation over. I want a drink before I die of dehydration."

"Sure, right of course"

Geordie, who liked his drink was already a few pints ahead of everyone and was well on his way, and losing money in the game machine.

"Bloody piece of shite, it's a rip off man."

"Well stop playing it then." Smudge suggested.

"Nah, it's gonna pay out in a minute I know it."

"A mugs game, come on sack it. We're going onto the club in a minute anyway."

"All reet, but I'm not happy. I've put fifteen quid in that frigging thing."

"Well quit before you lose anymore."

Geordie suckily came away from the machine.

"Anyone for another pint then?"

"I think Crysta and Gee are getting them in."

"Reet, I'll go give them a hand. Where's Seb?"

"Dunno, went over to the bar as well I think"

When Geordie walked off towards the bar it left just Smudge and Damien stood together by the fruit machine. There was an awkward silence apart from the music being played out into the pub. Eventually Damien asked "What's the dealio between Crysta and Seb then?"

"What as in are they a couple?"

Damien nodded in agreement

"Well they kinda are and kinda not. I wouldn't suggest you make a play for Crysta though if that's your intention."

"No, No. Just curious that's all. I think Gee might like her though."

"Hmm yeah, I've seen them talking an that. I'm sure Seb's clocked it as well."

"Can't see what the problem is if they're not an item."

"It's complicated mate, seriously. You're better off keeping out of it." Smudge said with conviction. With that Seb and Gee walked over.

"Where's the drinks mate?" Smudge asked

"We're sacking it. It's too busy in here. Come on lets go onto the club. Where is everyone?"

"Well Crysta is on her way over now and Geordie went looking for you. Oh no, here he is with some drinks."

"Here you go lads. Thought you were getting them in Seb."

"Yeah well I was getting ignored so I sacked it. We were going to move onto the club now anyway."

"You obviously don't have the Geordie charm. Come on then, get these drunk and we'll get gone."

"Damien, question for you" Crysta said pulling him to one side.

"Ok, what's up?"

"I've been wondering..you are obviously the son of the Devil. Sooo my question is. Who's your mum?"

This was not the question he was expecting. He was expecting her to ask why his dad had sent him up here to keep an eye on things, but not that. The drink had obviously made her forget about that for the moment. He just stood there silently looking at her. Crysta carried on, bridging the silence.

"Well you know some sort of act had to happen for you to be here. I'm just curious how it all, you know, came about?" The drinks had made it easier for Crysta to ask what she knew was a totally crazy question.

"Well" Damien started tentatively "As I understand it, when they accused the Pendle hill witches of fornicating with the Devil, they weren't wrong..if you know what I mean."

"What, really? One of the Pendle hill witches had sex with your dad and got pregnant with you. That's mental, who would have thought it. But that was like hundreds of years ago, you should be dead or really old, or somet," the alcohol making it harder for Crysta to process the information.

"I age differently to you. For a dog it's seven years to your one. I'm kinda the same but in reverse and it's more than seven years."

"So that would make you how old really?"

"I'm not sure. I've never done the maths. I lost track decades ago. I don't really care. I'm not even sure I've ever been asked before, how old I am, to be honest."

"Wow you don't have birthdays or owt then?"

"Crysta you know who my Dad is, a birthday is a nice thing. He doesn't do nice."

"Yeah good point, that's crazy though not knowing how old you are, jeez."

"What you guys talking about?" Seb asked coming over once he noticed they were having a cosy chat together.

"Oh nowt mate, come on drink up, let's get to the club before the queue gets too massive. I hate standing in queues, especially when you know the place you're queuing to get into isn't even all that good."

By the time they walked over to the club the queue was quite substantial. The floor was strewn with cigarette butts from where people had sparked up to relieve the boredom of the wait. The evening had grown chiller but at least it wasn't raining. Smudge lit a tab.

"Give me one of those Smudge."

"I didn't know you smoked." commented Gee

"She does after a few drinks don't ya Crysta. Those things will kill ya."

"No really, didn't know that." Crysta retorted back sarcastically.

"No need to bite my head off. Wow you are in a bad mood aren't you? Rag week this week is it?"

"No it's not in matter of fact. Why do you guys always assume that when a woman is in a bad mood it must be that's it because she's on. Have you ever thought it might just be because she is just in a bad mood? Now give me a smoke Smudge."

Smudge dutifully handed his tabs over to keep the peace and to avert the wrath of Crysta.

"You really are in a strop aren't you?"

"No I'm fine I just don't need a lecture on smoking from you, and my feet are killing me in these f'ing boots."

Just at this point they had reached the front of the queue. The bouncers were the usual big guys with wide shoulders that were probably more fat than muscle. Stood there with their black trousers, white shirts and the compulsory jacket that went down to the knee. It said I am a bouncer, look I have an ear piece and everything. Most of these guys were assholes that let the power of running a door go straight to their head. Moron's most of them, who probably didn't know any sort of martial art or how to defend themselves, relying on their size instead.

Lurch hadn't made it out that night as he was skint already. It was probably a good thing as his size always got attention from the bouncers. They always assumed that because he was a big lad that he was bound to come into the club and cause problems.

"Right you lot can go through, but not him" one of the bouncers with a dodgy goatee said, putting a hand on Damien's chest to stop his entrance."

"Why not?" Crysta exclaimed

"Because he has steel capped boots on, and I'll need ID from you as well lady."

"What are you kidding me? I'm twenty bloody seven; I've been coming to this club nearly every weekend."

"Yes well I don't like your attitude. No ID, no entry. As for him he's not coming in." he indicated to Damien.

"Hey guys I'm cool with this, I'll catch ya later ok." he flicked the cigarette he had lit while watching the proceedings at the bouncer's feet and stepped out of the queue. He headed towards the taxi rank that was conveniently situated across the road. He was slightly relieved. These were not his kind of people and he was pretty sure the club wouldn't play the sort of music that he liked. He wasn't too happy to be leaving Gee with Crysta though. What can he do tonight, he pondered. Nothing, it'll be fine. The name Gee aswell. Really imaginative..Not! What an idiot.

CHAPTER EIGHTEEN

"What do you mean she's gone?"

Damien was stood in his father's office getting grilled as his Dad looked like he was trying to create a groove into his expensive carpet with his pacing backwards and forwards.

"Well we went to a club and the bouncer wouldn't let me in because I had steel toe capped boots on. I got up this afternoon and both her and Gee had gone"

"Gee, who the bloody hell is Gee?"

"That's what Jesus is calling himself up there. Not that clever really is it?"

"Clever, I don't care about clever. What I care about son" the words were almost spat at him "is where they have gone to. In fact I can hazard a guess. Damn it, I'll never get her back now. You're a bloody idiot Damien you know that. I sent you up there to do one simple task and you well and truly messed it up."

"I'm sorry Dad, I didn't think he'd make his move so quickly."

"See that's the problem you didn't think. Now go, get out of my office, and get out of my sight."

Damien went to protest then thought better of it. Oh well back to my band practice. I didn't really care about this whole thing in the first place. He walked over the thick carpet and just as he pulled the door shut behind him he could hear his Dad give out a roar that shook the ground. Wow, he's really not happy.

Sam pulled himself together. He didn't like to show annoyance. Crysta going missing had created cracks in his usual calm exterior. There was only one way to confirm where she had gone. He had to go and check the vault.

The vault wasn't far from his office that overlooked the work area. The vault door arched across one side of a wall. It was immense. The black steel colour of the door made it almost melt out of sight and mix with the dimness of the surrounding corridor. If it wasn't for the large cogs and wheels which dominated the front of the door, you could nearly walk past it and not even see it.

Sam approached it and held up his hand towards the door. He closed his eyes and started to murmur under his breath, using a language nearly as old as the universe. His hand started to glow red and flames sparked out off of his fingertips. The cogs started to move. Some went clockwise, others anti clockwise. The sound of moving mechanics could be heard as things screeched and moved into their new position. Finally it went quiet. Sam opened his eyes. His hand returned to its usual form. The door opened up and he stepped inside. The door closing behind him almost the second he stepped inside.

The entire vault was bathed in a red glow. The sort of colour that photographers use when developing their photos. Before him were rows upon rows of shelves. Each shelf contained thousands upon thousands of scrolls. Each scroll had the signed signature of each soul that he possessed. If Crysta had been taken to where he thought, it would be gone. He closed his eyes again. There was a whooshing sound and the feel of a breeze move past his face. When he opened his eyes again one of the shelves had moved along to contain the scrolls starting with S. He walked forward to where Crysta's scroll should be. It was as he thought, gone.

The roar he gave out this time shook the tables of all the people whose eternity was to be sat at a desk. Pencils rolled onto the floor and cups full of coffee rippled and spilt. People stopped what they were doing and looked at each other. They all guessed that someone must have annoyed the Boss again.

CHAPTER NINETEEN

It was about 2am before Seb realised that he hadn't seen Crysta or Gee for that matter. Geordie was stood at the bar next to him barely able to keep himself upright. Smudge had gone home about an hour ago as his success at pulling had drawn a blank. He wanted a kebab and to get back and crash out. Crysta had met up with some other girls from camp and was on the dance floor last time Seb had seen her, dancing to some cheesy pop songs. That was the thing that Crysta had found when you come out with blokes. They don't dance, they just generally prop up a bar or hang around a table. Dancing got in the way of drinking. It's only when they had drunk enough that they danced. By then they didn't care about how stupid they may look.

How long ago was that I saw her, he mused. He turned to Geordie "Did you see whether Crysta went off anywhere with Gee?"

"What mate?" Geordie slurred, not being able to hear over the music.

"Crysta, have you seen her or Gee anywhere?" Seb shouted in his ear.

Geordie just shook his head, speaking comprehensively was becoming a problem. Seb could feel a little bit of anger starting to build. How dare she. I can't believe she went off with him without at least saying something to me first. She probably knew how I'd react. Still, and him, that bloody

Gee. He said he wasn't interested, just making polite conversation he said. Right I'm going back to camp and I'm going to confront them.

"Right Geordie come on lets go."

"Where we gannin like, to the kebab shop. I could murder a kebab."

"No back to camp."

"What nah kebab, ha way man. I need a kebab. Nowt like left over kebab for breakfast when you're hung over."

"Right fine, come on then get ya self together, we're going now. Don't make me have to carry you either."

"What?"

"I said don't, oh forget it." Seb walked off with Geordie staggering in tow.

It was nearly 3 am by the time they got back to the camp. The taxi drivers weren't allowed to drive onto the camp so walking up the hill to the block was a long process with Geordie taking one step forward and three steps back. He literally fell into a bush at one point. All Seb could see was one half of Geordie in the bush and one half out, his right arm raised in the air to rescue his kebab from the fall. Seb grabbed his upraised arm and pulled him upright.

"Come on you drunken idiot."

When Seb eventually got back to the block he made sure Geordie got to his room ok. He dived almost face first onto the bed the minute his door was opened and didn't move. Seb took the untouched Kebab out of his hand and put it on the side. Rolled him onto his front, just in case he puked, and left the room. He stood in the the corridor for a moment to gather his thoughts. What if I barge into her room and they are having sex, then what. They could be in his room. Shall I just leave it? He was quite riled up by the whole thing and he was sure that if he went to his room and tried to ignore it, the whole thing would play on his mind until he at least spoke to Crysta. He made the decision and walked out of the corridor through the double doors and across the concrete square towards the female accommodation.

He paused for a second outsider her door, he put his ear up against it to see if could hear anything that might give away what could be going on inside. Nothing, he couldn't hear anything. They must have gone to his. He tapped lightly on the door just in case.

"Crysta" he whispered "Are you in, I want to talk." No response.

"Look Crysta even if he's in there with you, just come out, I just want a chat" Nothing. Right either she's ignoring me or they are over at his. He placed his ear up to the door to confirm that he couldn't hear any movement on the other side. When all was still quiet he turned away and made his way back over to the male accommodation.

Smudge was still up watching TV with his door open when he walked past

"Hello mate what you up to? Did I miss anything when I left?"

"Not really."

"Where are you going?"

"I've just come to have a word with Gee."

"I haven't seen him come past. Didn't he not come back with you then?"

"No, Crysta and Gee have disappeared somewhere."

"Oh" was all Smudge could say when the comprehension of what that could mean sunk in. Then he added "Have you tried Crysta's room?"

"Yes, I've just come from there." Seb replied irritably.

"Well I don't think they are in his room. I haven't seen either of them go past since I came back. They were still in the club with you when I left." there was no reply from Seb. He was glaring at Gee's door almost willing it to open on its own.

"I mean even if they are, and you go barging in there. What are you planning to do?" Smudge continued.

"I dunno. Speak to Crysta. Ask her what she's doing with that idiot. I'm not sure."

"Well leave it for now. Don't be getting into a big barney tonight. Go get your head down and catch up and speak to Crysta later. They may have come back separately for all you know."

"Well if Crysta wanted to go why didn't she come and tell me she was leaving. She knows I would have left with her."

"Maybe she couldn't find ya mate. Look it's probably not what you think. Leave it eh, sort it out in the morning."

"Yeah right. You're right." He took another glance at Gee's door that was still resolutely shut and walked to his room.

He sat on his bed with his head in his hands. No, he reassured himself, it's probably not what I think. I'll speak to Crysta later. He lay down and was quickly asleep on top of his covers fully clothed. The amount of alcohol he had consumed, that had been kept at bay with his stressing over Crysta and Gee finally catching up. His digital clock next to him glowed red, its digits showing 04.15am.

CHAPTER TWENTY ONE

Gee was sat on the toilet with the seat down in the club. The place stank and there was bits of loo roll on the floor that threatened to attach itself to the nearest shoe it could find so you could make an embarrassing entrance back into the club with it stuck to the bottom.

He put his hands together in prayer. He whispered under his breath

"Right I know you know that Damien is here. That means Sam has something planned. I need to make my move now while he's not here. He wasn't allowed in the club because he had steel toe cap boots on. Not sure why I told you that I'm sure you're aware of that already. Ok so I just need to know how I'm supposed to get her to you." He wasn't expecting a booming voice but he was hoping for something. An idea to be planted into his head, a sign of some sort, just something. He was getting zip, apart from the sounds of drunken guys urinating and mostly missing and hitting the floor.

He continued "Come on give me an idea, anything." He looked up at the ceiling that was a garish blue colour. When nothing seemed to be forthcoming he stood up and went out of the stall and over to the mirrors. They were all covered in water spray and the end sink was blocked with paper and was close to over flowing. Paper towels were strewn across the top, soaked and squeezed into sodden balls. Jesus washed his hands and looked across at a poster that caught his eye. It read 'Go for the lite' it was advertising Lite Beer. Go for the light, does that mean something. Take

Crysta towards the light, what light though? Jesus processed the idea in his head. Right I'm going to find Crysta, and then I'm going to find the brightest disco light and hope I'm right. If I'm not, we're going to get dazzled and walk straight into a high watt bulb. I'm pretty sure Crysta won't thank me for that.

"Um Gee, where am I exactly? I've got a white spots in my eyes that won't go away even when I blink" Crysta exclaimed.

"What can you remember?"

"You, coming up to me in the club, taking me by the arm and dragging me towards a light that was next to the stage near the DJ. That's it. I can't hear music anymore so I'm obviously not in the club. So I say again, where am I?"

"You're in Heaven"

"What? Shut up, are you taking the mickey? You are aren't you? I've passed out from being drunk and this is a dream right?"

"Does it feel like a dream?"

Things were starting to come back into focus and all Crysta could see now was some lift doors with mirrors either side. There were some comfy chairs and a table with some magazines on it. Everywhere else just seemed white for miles and miles.

"Well it does seem real but, how, why? Why have you brought me here? You obviously don't work for the Boss then, You! You must work for the main man then. So you must be" she paused as her brain processed everything "Jesus, your Jesus aren't you?"

"You've asked a lot of questions there Crysta. I'll let the main man, as you call him, answer most of them, but yes I am Jesus."

"Jesus Christ!"

"Yes"

"No I meant, I was blaspheming, forget it, it doesn't matter. I thought you looked familiar but I just couldn't put my finger on it. This is crazy. I'm really in heaven. So why have you brought me here?" Crysta paused and looked around " So when you come up to heaven aren't you supposed to be greeted like, by all of your family and pets that have, you know, passed on?"

"I'm sure you'll catch up with them eventually. This wasn't exactly a scheduled pick up. You were meant to come here ten years ago."

"10 yrs ago, but that was when I signed up with you know who." Crysta tried to make sense of it all and decided she couldn't so she completed her sentence by saying "I'm confused. I don't get it."

"Like I said I'll let the Guv fill in all the details, first of all I think a certain dog has come up to greet you."

Crysta turned around to see Prince coming out of the white and running towards her. No sign of problems in his hips at all. She instantly went down on one knee and hugged his head, his coat soft on her skin. She could feel a lump start to build in her throat and tears come to her eyes. Prince licked her face excitedly.

"I can feel." she said to Jesus

"I feel happy, I'm crying. What happened? Am I whole again?" She stood up and looked quizzically at Jesus while Prince bounded around, bum in the air, tail wagging, showing the classic dog sign of play with me.

"When you come to heaven, everyone has their soul. By being here it's been returned to you."

Crysta just stood frozen for a moment, letting the information digest. After ten years she could feel again. The part of her that had been missing for all that time, back inside her. Her soul. She felt like crying again.

"So what happens now? Was that why you were sent? To rescue me and my soul? Well thanks, I really appreciate it. So how does it work now then?

I take it I don't work for him anymore. I can live my life normally again. How do I get back down?" Realising that Crysta wasn't going to give him any more attention for the moment, Prince had wondered over to one of the chairs to relieve himself. He didn't have too, it was just a habit.

Jesus just looked at Crysta. She had a slightly scared look on her face and was asking a lot of questions. He knew that she probably had a hundred more which he was going to leave to the Guv to answer. The answer to the last question however, he thought it only fair to tell her. Even though he knew for sure that she wasn't going to like what he was going to say.

"You don't go back Crysta, this is it. You're here for good now. Like you were meant to be all those years ago."

CHAPTER TWENTY TWO

Seb woke up Sunday afternoon with a hangover and the feeling that something wasn't quite right, apart from his stomach and head. He'd had the most vivid dream about a girl called Crysta. They were best of mates, or were they an item. He wasn't sure. The food in the cookhouse was being cooked by a guy who looked remarkably like Jesus but without the beard and long hair. There was also this strange guy whose fringe was far too long to be acceptable by Army standards. He had steel toe capped boots on and the blackest pupils he had ever seen. He took an aspirin or two and hoped they would help get the haunting dream out of his mind. It seemed like it had been so real.

Monday morning was squadron PT. Always a nice way to start the week. They had circuits this morning and the PTI had obviously decided that he hated Mondays as much as Garfield and was going to take it out on everyone else.

The idea of circuits was so that you worked every muscle in your body and also the ones you didn't know you had. They had to do heaves, also known as chin ups. People were currently hanging onto the bar and kicking their legs frantically hoping the momentum would somehow get their chin over the top of the bar. As their chin got nearer the top, you could see them with their head right back, eyes bulging and arms screaming and the PTI kindly screaming "that if you didn't get your bloody chin over that bar then he would shove a rocket up your arse to help you."

You had various tortures with benches. Step ups. Straddle jumps, which were when you were stood with the bench in between your legs, then you had to jump both feet onto the bench at the same time. Tricep dips, legs out straight, hands on the bench and you had to dip most of your body weight.

The usual sit ups where you were informed by the PTI that you had to keep doing until <u>his</u> stomach hurt. Press ups, which the PTI always enjoyed pointing out that if you went onto your knees during press ups you were obviously a girlie and should wear a dress and call yourself Dorris. Sprints up and down the hall where the PTI would scream at you to work your legs and "move, move, move!!" Everything had to be done with the speed of a thousand Gazelles. No one knew how fast that was but they guessed that it was pretty quick, and they no matter how much the PTI yelled at them were not going to be able to go that quickly. It didn't stop the PTI trying to make them anyway. The medicine ball press was hated by everyone who had weak upper body strength. You had to push the med ball straight out horizontal to your body then bring it back in again and take it up over your head as quickly as possible. Of course there were squat thrust but with the added bonus of having to jump up afterwards bringing your knees up to your chest. This was also called 'bastard with a jump' and of course star jumps. Not ordinary star jumps though, of course, can't have anything too easy. You had to put your hands on the floor and then jump spreading your arms and legs out like a star. Not only did you look stupid doing it but it was tiring after a while. All of it was.

The PTI always made it a minute at each station on the first circuit round. Then after one complete circuit you started again and he reduced the time down to forty five seconds per station. Then down to thirty seconds per station on the third time round. Then it was cool down. If the PTI was feeling in a particularly nasty mood, they would go round a fourth time and it would be back to a minute each station again. This was about the time where people would be waiting for the PTI to have his back to them so they could stop doing whatever activity they were in the middle of and catch a quick break. Skive to survive it was called. Then when the PTI would look in their direction again they would re start the activity again with great effort like they were doing it like that the whole time.

It was during this time at the sit up station that Seb asked Jon boy

"Did we ever have a girl based here called Crysta?"

"Can't talk mate, I'm literally hanging out of my hoop. I can never understand why sit ups hurt my neck and legs more than my stomach."

"Oy you two ladies over there chatting. If you have the energy to talk you aren't working hard enough. That's an extra twenty seconds added lads. I'm sure the rest of the group will thank you for that" the PTI yelled across the hall.

There were general moans and groans around the hall. The PTI blew his whistle and screeched in a high pitch tone "Change" which indicated to people that they should move onto the next station. Everyone dropped, fell and crawled themselves onto the next piece of torture.

Only bloody PTI's would get a kick from stuff like this, Seb thought as he tried to push the med ball out, with their stupid red shorts, normally too tight, and white vest tops with those red crossed swords on them. They only wear vest tops to show off their muscled arms. Posers the lot of them.

"What I don't get about PTI's is that we have to call them Staff, no matter what rank they are." Lurch said once they had finally got into the changing rooms. It was your typical changing room. Benches with hooks above them, a couple of toilet stalls and six shower heads on the back wall. When you're in the Army, seeing people naked is normal.

"It's because we're supposed to respect them for being PTI's and completing a hard course or somet, not sure really." Geordie added.

"Well correct me if I'm wrong." Seb interjected "They volunteer for the course, they want to get beasted. So why should we call them staff because of that?"

"I'm not even sure that's the proper reason. Don't be biting my head off. It's not my fault their all spanners." Geordie answered to try and defend his comment.

"They're sadists" Lurch pointed out.

"Spot on Lurch my friend they are" then he did a double take just to check it was actually Lurch that had said such an astute thing, then continued on his tirade "Bloody sadists the lot of them. They love to get tortured and to torture others. I hate it when we're on boot runs with 35kilos of weight, boots, helmet, weapon, the full monty and those tossers are running next to you with combat trousers and those stupid vest tops not carrying any kit at all. I hate them." Seb said with venom in his tone.

"I remember when a PTI grabbed the back of my Bergen once and tried to drag me up with him. Stay with me he kept saying pointing down to his side. If I wasn't so tired I would have knocked him out" Smudge decided to share with everyone.

"I hate it when they do that. I was physically throwing up once and they were still trying to drag me along." Geordie said "I had been drinking the night before mind so I was feeling a little bit rough."

"Tossers the lot of them." Seb repeated, while dragging his boot on with a bit more force than necessary "I mean all that bull they yell at you, do you think they learn that on the course. Have a little book of stupid comments that they have to learn and then get tested on the next day. I mean, what does do sit ups until his own stomach hurts, even mean. It's impossible. It's always just over that hill or around that tree, which is guaranteed to be a good mile away."

"You're in a right ole mood today mate." Smudge noted.

"Yeah well I haven't been sleeping too well lately. I keep having this vivid dream about a girl called Crysta. Does that name ring a bell with any of you?"

"I don't think I want to talk to you about your wet dreams mate I haven't had breakfast yet." was Smudges response.

"No seriously does anyone recognise the name? There was also a guy who looked like Jesus that cooked the most amazing food in the cookhouse."

"Amazing food in the cookhouse, made by a guy who looked like Jesus. Doesn't that make it obvious that it was clearly a dream? We don't care about your weird dreams. You'll be trying to tell us our horoscopes next. Come on and get your shit together and let's get some scoff. We'll have to try and get some beans before they all get stuck together on the tray and start screaming for help." Jon boy told Seb.

"We were like beans in that PT session." Lurch added into the conversation. Everyone stopped to look at him for an explanation of his statement "We were screaming for help, you said that the beans were stuck together and screamin'."

"Ok Lurch we get it very good." Seb cut him off "Come on lets go" he grabbed his beret off the hook and headed to the door "So no one knows any bird called Crysta then?"

"No man. Will you shut up about your imaginary girlfriend, you're doing my head in." was the last comment that could be heard from Jon Boy as the door to the changing room closed behind them.

CHAPTER TWENTY-THREE

Sky was now a copper living outside Birmingham in a place called Telford. Sky shared a house with another female copper friend. They had gone through training together and they both specified that they didn't mind which area they worked in once they qualified. So Birmingham it was. There was always something going on by the Bull ring shopping centre. Racial attacks were quite common, especially when people had been drinking.

None of this mattered to Sky tonight; she was going to see the psychic Colin Fry with her house mate Leah. It was their days off. They worked shifts in their job but they were always required to come in and do additional shifts as they were always short of manpower. They had booked these tickets months previously and even put in leave for it to make sure they wouldn't get called back to work.

Ever since her sister Crysta had died in the car accident she had been to see a few mediums and tried to get contact with her. Sky was told by one particular medium at a fair that her sister's soul was missing and she was drifting around lost. This, as you can imagine, upset Sky immensely and she had stopped trying to find Crysta for a long time. When Leah had suggested going to see Colin Fry, Sky was reluctant at first. Leah pointed out that compared to a probable hack at some fair, that someone famous like Colin Fry would be her best chance of speaking to Crysta.

Sky had rang her parents to tell them she was going. Her mum liked to believe that there was something more and told her to ring if anyone did come through. Obviously they all hoped Crysta would. Even the Dad, forever the sceptic, secretly hoped his little girl would come through. Crysta was never quiet in life he thought; I'm surprised that she's been able to stay quiet in death.

As Sky was getting dressed she remembered a conversation herself and Crysta had once while watching Most Haunted on telly. Kieran O'Keefe was the man on the show who was supposed to find logical explanation for everything that occurred on the show. He wondered around with alarms and heat devices, and put every noise down to the building being old and groaning. Crysta had said to Sky that if she was a ghost she would find Kieran during one of the shows and yell stuff in his ear or pull on his clothes.

"It would be funny to see him try and pass that off as a creaking building" Crysta had said.

The thought made Sky smile. Sky never really felt like Crysta had gone. In her head she felt like she had only spoken to her a couple of days previously. It was ten years ago. Surely not, it couldn't have been that long since she last spoke to her sister. There was something niggling her and she couldn't put her finger on it. A voice in the back of her head kept saying ,she never died in that crash, she's only been gone for a couple of days, hasn't she?

Sky shook her head, it's not possible but it just feels that it's right. Sky remembered her funeral, the tears and the pain of herself and the family. All of Crysta's friends had come, the crematorium was full. Yet in the last couple of days it didn't seem right. Something had changed and she suddenly had a good feeling about tonight. Crysta was going to come through, she knew. Sky crossed her fingers and gave a glance heavenwards just in case.

A shout from Leah brought her out of her reverie. Sky took one last look in the mirror. Even though there was two years difference between her and Crysta they had looked quite similar. Sky always had a bit of comfort in knowing that how she looked was probably similar as to how Crysta would look if she was alive. Well Crysta would probably have less grey hair. Curse of the Sloane family female to go grey early.

Another yell from down the stairs. "Coming" Sky called back down.

As they pulled out of the drive Sky turned to Leah and said

"You know I have a really good feeling about tonight."

"Yeah, good. I've got my fingers crossed for you mate." Leah replied just as a Mettalica song came on the radio, it was Enter Sandman.

"Man, I haven't heard this in years. I used to listen to this with Crysta. She learnt all the words. It annoyed me at the time because it was my music and she didn't even like it. Wierd that it's playing now don't you think?" Sky asked Leah quizzically

"What do you think it's some kind of omen or somet, dunno, it does seem a little wierd. Maybe your little sister is trying to get through early."

"Yeah I hope so. Wouldn't that be great?"

CHAPTER TWENTY-FOUR

Crysta had sat on one of the chairs next to the lift. Prince had settled across in front of her feet, sensing a change of mood in Crysta.

"So I'm dead, this is it, I have to stay here forever?" Crysta turned to look at Jesus for an answer.

"You say it like it's a bad thing. It's amazing up here. You can speak to Elvis, Marilyn Monroe or even Princess Diana. Find out if she was really pregnant or not when she died, or whether she was murdered. Psychics on earth have been trying to contact them for years to find out the answer to questions like that. You can ask them yourself first hand. Some people would die to be in your shoes" he realised what he said "You know what I mean" he finished desperately.

"What about my family, my friends. Seb and the guys?"

"Seb and the guys won't remember you Crysta. You died at seventeen so you never joined the Army or served with them. That's how your family will remember it also. They may have some residual memory of say speaking to you yesterday. The will discount it though obviously. In time it will have always been that you died when you did. No one will remember that you actually walked around on Earth for another ten years after. All be it with no soul. Don't you feel better now you have had your soul restored to you?"

"I suppose so. My family though, I didn't even get to say goodbye or anything."

"Not many people get the chance to do so before they die Crysta. You can go down and visit them though in spirit form. They obviously won't hear or see you but you may find some comfort in going down and seeing what their up to. You can do that anytime you want."

"What like haunt them?"

"Not really. You're not an Earth bound spirit; you can go down in visitation."

"Wow that is the best news I've had since I got here. Right so how do I get down? In one of those lifts?"

"No they lead to the Guvs office. Speaking of which I should send you up to him. He'll be expecting you. I'm sure you have some questions for him. I warn you though it's a quite a journey"

Crysta started absentmindedly stroking Prince, who took full advantage and rolled onto his back so his stomach would get stroked.

"I'm going to be here for all eternity right, so going to see the Guv can wait. I want to go down and visit now. While someone may still remember that I was only just down there" she paused and looked at herself and Gee. They were still wearing the clothes they had been wearing when they went out to the club. At least I shaved my legs and armpits. I'm not stuck up in Heaven for all eternity with hairy legs and wearing bad clothes. Crysta remembered asking her sister to make sure that she was hair free if she died. Imagine being in Heaven and having hairy legs or pits and not being able to shave them. They had laughed at the time. If her sister's recollection now was that she died 10yrs ago, I wonder if she checked my legs. I doubt it. It seemed a stupid thought now she was up here. You could be how you wanted up here. Hair free, pain free or even fat free if wanted. It was Heaven after all.

"I'm not sure the Guv would be happy with that." Gee said interrupting her thoughts.

"No I guess you're right, um what is that running towards us? Is that a cherub? Oh my, they look just as I thought they would."

Prince rolled back onto his feet and started yapping excitedly at the new addition to the group. The cherub handed a piece of paper to Gee nodded his head towards Crysta, then ran back the way he came. Crysta watched fascinated.

"Why give them wings that will never be able to fly with. I suppose if they lost some weight it may just work."

"The Guv is a traditionalist Crysta. However you perceived Heaven to be is exactly how it will be" he turned his attention to the paper he had been given. It was an e-mail from the Guv. It read...

> Allow Crysta to do what she feels she needs to do right now. Show her how. I will see her when she is ready. I have waited many years to speak to her. What are a few more days. Her sister is attending a psychic meeting tonight. Get her there.
>
> God

"Right Crysta change of plan, apparently your sister is going to see a psychic tonight. The Guv told me to get you down there so you can see and speak to her. If you would like that?"

"What!" Crysta said jumping to her feet "Are you kidding, I would love that."

"Right how are you on heights?"

CHAPTER TWENTY-FIVE

Sky and Leah arrived at the theatre that was hosting Colin Fry. It was in the Place Theatre in Oakengates, so the drive wasn't too bad. The last time Sky had been there was to watch the Rocky horror picture show. Sky and Leah were some of the few people who hadn't dressed up and they regretted it. Standing in the house previously discussing whether they should put on stocking and suspenders, then walk through the streets, just seemed like the most absurd idea. Once there and surrounded by people dressed up in the most garish costumes, Sky and Leah stood out a mile in their ordinary jeans and T-shirt. As they took their seats in the theatre Sky had a flash back of when the gentleman next to her, dressed up in fish nets, full make up, wig and Basque, complained during the show that one of his balloon breasts had burst. Leah reminded her that while doing the time warp stood on the self folding chairs that Sky had lost one of her legs down the back of her seat as the chair tried to put itself away, with her still stood on it. They giggled like little school girls at the memory, getting looks from the stern grey haired lady in front of them, probably hoping her husband would make an appearance.

They gave each other sheepish grins and then settled down. The theatre had placed up a huge screen in front of the red curtains. A camera was set up on either side of the stage. Whatever the camera saw was being reflected out onto the screen, this way everyone could clearly see the psychic and also anyone in the audience that Colin was relaying a message to. The theatre was packed but the lights didn't dim as Colin came out on stage, they stayed on so everyone could see each other better. This was weird at first as it always customary for the audience to be in the dark.

He started by telling people who he was, like people who paid to go and see him wouldn't know, but Sky guessed there were probably a few people who had been dragged along by their partners. He told the audience about his gift and how long he had been working for. He also invited anyone who was even a little bit sceptical to leave. He knew he had the gift and wasn't there to prove anything to them. He did these tours to help people who genuinely believed and wanted to get in touch with their loved ones.

He looks exactly like he does on the telly Sky thought, Slim, average height, thinning brown hair and very obviously gay. He later mentioned that he was and Sky gave herself a mental tap on the back that her 'gaydar' was still working.

He then went very quickly into his readings and the people he picked up and spoke to always seemed to relate to what he was telling them about the person and nine times out of ten there were tears. Sky had to check herself a few times. A young teenage boy had come through who had died in a car accident. Colin said that the teenager, called Paul was quite happy to be stood on stage next to him and to be seeing his Mum and sister again. Still it was hard not to feel the relief of the family that they are getting to hear that their loved ones are happy and fine, but also the realisation that they won't be able to speak to them properly again. It was an emotionally charged atmosphere.

"Ok I've now got a teenage female coming through; she's just watched how Paul came through and is following his lead. I'm getting the letter C for her first name."

Sky almost sat up bolt right and Leah gave her a look that said it may be just wait a moment.

"Now I'm getting mixed signals with this person, I feel she has only just recently left this plain, but I also getting that she may have been lost to this world a long time ago. Wait she's trying to explain." Colin continued. He paused for a moment and scanned around the audience. "This person,

I think her name is Crysta is saying her sister is in middle on the raised seating, row C."

The camera man swung his camera in the direction ordered and started sweeping across where Sky and Leah were sat. Sky was sat looking stunned for a moment and Leah was trying to encourage her to put up her hand to indicate that she may be the person Colin was looking for.

"If the name Crysta rings any bells in that area can you please let me know, she's adamant that her sister, Sky is here."

Leah frustrated that Sky wasn't responded grabbed Sky's arm and pushed it into the air. Suddenly both Sky and Leah were on the large screen and a member of Colin's team was pushing a microphone into her hand.

"Is your name Sky?" Colin asked a still very stunned Sky.

"Ah huh" was all she could manage.

"This lady coming through, is the name Crysta right?"

"Uh huh"

"Can you tell me how long ago she passed away as I'm getting confused signals on the details but I do know she was hit by a car, am I right?"

"Uh yes a car. It was ten years ago."

"Yes, she is really trying to get a message to you but it isn't making any sense at the moment. If I'm right Crysta is saying that she has only got her soul back and hasn't been in Heaven long. You can see why I'm confused then Sky as you are telling me that she died ten years ago. Wait she's trying to tell me more." Colin paused for a moment and stood as if he was trying to listen to someone that no one else could see.

"She asked me whether you remember that she used to work for a dark lord, and you would remember what that meant. Well until only a couple of days ago she did but now she has been brought to Heaven. Does any of that make sense?"

"Not really no, I'm sorry."

"Well you are the right person I know that but it's like the message is getting scrambled. Crysta is saying now and quite loudly in my ear, don't forget me and love to Mum and Dad. Also that Prince is up there with her."

"Prince was our German Shepherd dog, he passed away a few months ago" Sky informed him glad to get some information that made sense and confirmed to her that is was definitely Crysta coming through. Sky could feel her stomach turn into a knot and her eyes were stinging.

"Crysta seems to be going now so I leave her love with you. God Bless."

The rest of the night went with a blur. The car journey home Sky and Leah tried to analyze what Colin had said. Sky still couldn't figure out the dark lord message. It was only when she went to bed that it came to her in a dream. Sky was sitting in her room surrounded by her Iron Maiden pictures and Crysta was telling her how she worked for the Devil now. She had no soul but it was ok as she didn't die in the car accident. It gave her more time on Earth to spend with her and her parents. The last thing Sky remembered before going into a dreamless sleep was Crysta asking her to find a man called Tumble.

CHAPTER TWENTY-SIX

Crysta had been taken to what Gee called the visiting room. Initially as she approached it looked like a swimming pool full of clouds. The edge of the pool was a wall sitting approx 5 layers of brick high. The pool was so expanse that Crysta could only see two edges and one corner. One was running the width and the other the length. The three other corners couldn't be seen.

Jesus led Crysta over to the wall and looked over into the expanse of swimming clouds. Crysta sat next to him

"The entire floor here is made of clouds. So why the wall?"

"This area is special. It's where you come to observe or join your family or friends. You have to imagine where you want to go, part the clouds and you will be above the person you wish to visit. Then you step down to join them. Watch that young man over there. He is going to the same place as you."

Crysta looked up to see the young lad. She hadn't noticed him before but as she looked around she saw not only him but hundreds of people moving in and out of the clouds. In the distance people were only shadows. Further away all that could be seen were where the clouds were being disturbed and wisps were being moved into unusual shapes that soon settled back down to the surface.

The young lad parted the surface, stepped over the edge then disappeared.

"Woh, where's he gone?"

"He is now on stage next to Colin Fry. Obviously no one can see him and only Colin will be able to hear him. It's still tough to get through though. He may figuratively be stood next to him but he is still has all the distance from here to get himself heard. It's tough for the psychics. Colin is one of the good ones."

"Ok so all I have to do is just wave a gap in the clouds then step onto the stage." As she asked this Crysta swept her hand over the clouds but when they parted it wasn't the stage she saw. Crysta gasped and jumped up from the wall.

"Woh what the hell am I looking at here? Is this like the universe or something?"

Swimming below her was a sea of black, dotted with stars and Crysta could see at least two or three planets. One was bright red.

"Is that Mars? Mars is red right?"

Jesus looked over to where Crysta had parted the clouds.

"No this isn't even part of your solar system. This is way beyond your furthest known planet. Heaven covers the whole universe, not just your little patch of sky."

Crysta sat back down again. Seeing that open up in front of her eyes had given her the feeling you get when you're on a roller coaster and it's just about to drop you down the first hill.

"Wow that's amazing. You could have warned me though; I nearly had a heart attack. I thought you said that I would see the stage."

"You would have if you had visualised it first, not steam straight in."

"This is amazing though. Wow it's like being in a space ship. So if I was to step in now what would happen? Would I just drift around? Lost in space."

"You wouldn't be able to step down into this; it's only earth bound solid places. You can try and step onto it but you'll be stood on an invisible see through floor. Want to try?"

"Hmm I'm not sure. I'm not scared of heights or owt but, I dunno. It's a bit like going out onto that corridor they have built out onto the Grand Canyon."

"Have you done that then?" Jesus enquired

"Well no, but I've seen pictures. I can imagine that would make your stomach jolt at first when you first step onto that floor."

Crysta swung her legs over the edge and put a tentative toe towards the vast star strewn vastness below her. It dipped slightly then stopped as if hitting something solid. She brought her other foot over so that it was next to the other one. Crysta still placed it carefully, still not trusting one hundred per cent that it wasn't going to suddenly fall into the atmosphere below. The floor remained solid with stars and planets whirling beneath them. Crysta tapped her toes a couple of times to test the sturdiness. Ready to pull her feet back over the wall in an instant should the floor suddenly show any sign of weakness. Jesus observed it all with interest.

"Have you ever done this?" Crysta suddenly asked him.

"Of course. Also it took me a while to build up to it so don't worry."

As if the verification that Gee had done it and that she was going to be ok, Crysta stood up. It did have that effect. As she looked down into the universe her stomach and heart tried to have a race to jump out of her.

"This has got to be one of the maddest things I've ever done" Crysta was stood frozen to the spot as the clouds closed in around her feet and the sights below could no longer be seen"

"Well done Crysta, I'm impressed. It took me decades to get the courage up to do that. Come sit back down."

Crysta more turned and sat down on the spot rather than walk over to the wall, abruptly pulling her legs over. Crysta realised that she was placing them down on a floor this side that was just covered in clouds.

"I've been walking on clouds the whole time I've been here. It hasn't occurred to me that I may fall through once yet. Until now."

"It's best not to think about it too hard. Right let's get you onto that stage before the show finishes. Now concentrate this time. Imagine Colin Fry stood on stage." he looked at Crysta.

"Right you got that picture in your head?"

Crysta nodded

"Ok now try."

Crysta swept her hands over the clouds and this time they did in fact part to an aerial view of Colin Fry.

"This is bizarre." Crysta remarked.

"Yep no time to dwell on it, over you go."

"What. It's still a hell of a drop to the stage."

"Look Crysta it's not like you're going to hurt yourself. You're dead remember, now come on. He's trying to locate someone now and you don't want him to tune in on someone else. Now go."

Crysta looked at him with slight panic but pushed herself off the edge anyway; as if she was lowering herself into a swimming pool that she thought would either be cold or worse, have a shark in it.

The clouds enveloped her at first. There was no feeling of floating or even falling. When she came out of the clouds she was just there, next to Colin.

What incurred next was the most infuriating five minutes of Crysta's life. It was like trying to communicate to someone through a badly tuned radio. The volume came in and out. Crysta couldn't always hear what he was saying, and based on the stuff he was saying to her sister, he couldn't hear her properly either.

'Well this is a waste of time' Crysta thought. Crysta looked out to where her sister was sat and couldn't help tears suddenly spring to her eyes. Crysta turned to Colin and yelled,

"Tell her not to forget me and love to Mum and Dad. Also that Prince is up here with me."

This message at least seemed to have got through as Sky seemed to have a look of relief on her face on hearing about Prince. Sky also looked a little sad.

'It sucks she thinks I'm dead. I only spoke to her a couple of days ago' Crysta thought. It was too late to tell Colin anything else. Crysta was being pulled up again and was emerging back into the visiting room. Crysta walked back over to the wall with a bit more confidence this time.

"Well" she said to Gee, who was still sat there "that was a complete waste of time."

"Not completely. At least you tried. Now come on, time to meet the Guv."

"Oh what seriously? Just let me drop in on one other person first."

Jesus hesitated but saw the imploring look in Crysta's eyes.

"Ok but don't take long. I'll meet you in the waiting lounge where you came in once you've done ok."

"Ok, cheers Gee you're star."

CHAPTER TWENTY-SEVEN

Seb was sat on the throne, flicking through one of the Nuts magazine. A noise outside made him look up and he waited to see if anyone was about to speak to him. When it stayed quiet he returned his attention back to the magazine. He heard a tap coming on this time.

"Hey who's out there? Can't a guy shit in peace round here?"

There was still no reply. Seb placed the magazine down and tried to look under the door to see if he could see feet. He couldn't, but the room was beginning to steam up. Someone had obviously put the hot tap on for a joke and then legged it.

Ha bloody ha, Seb thought, Yeah that's really funny.

Still convinced that someone could be hiding in another stall, when he came out into the bathroom he did it slowly. Ready to pounce on the first person he saw. There was no one in the immediate area. He searched the other two stalls, the shower and bath area. Nothing just a room full of steam and the sound of the running tap. Seb pulled the door into the corridor open and yelled

"Ha Ha very funny" just in case someone was behind their door giggling at their little joke then came back in to turn the tap off. As he approached the tap he suddenly noticed writing in the mirror. It read

Seb it's me Crysta, I know you remember me

"Bloody hell" Seb exclaimed. He did remember Crysta but the other guys didn't seem to, so he stopped mentioning her. "I bloody knew it" he said to the empty bathroom.

"So where are you, what's with all this writing on mirrors and stuff?"

As he looked around he saw more writing appear but no person there to do the writing. His heart almost stopped and he froze to the spot.

"Come on Crysta this isn't funny you're freaking me out."

The new message read:

You've seen the film Ghost, this was the only way I could think of speaking to you

"What so you're like dead. It doesn't make sense. I remember you. I worked with you, I lo" he stopped himself from finishing the sentence, and then continued "Even if you died recently, why can't the others remember you. None of this is making sense." he watched as the invisible hand of Crysta wrote on the mirror again.

It's a long story Seb and I don't have enough mirrors. I did live. Find my sister she remembers me

She scribbled her sister's number on the last mirror then felt the pull again. There must be a time limit Crysta thought as she drifted up looking down on Seb. He was frozen to the spot.

Crysta giggled as she thought that she has probably scared the bejeezers out of him. Writing on mirrors, she mused, is much more effective than mediums.

Crysta had emerged back into the visiting room. She quickly stepped over the wall then parted the clouds again to see what Seb was doing. It went straight to the bathroom again.

I'm getting the hang of this, Crysta told herself smugly. The bathroom was empty and the tap was still on. Then Seb came rushing back in with a pad and pen. He started furiously scribbling Sky's number down. He then turned off the tap and just looked around in amazement. The messages in the mirrors could still been seen. Shaking his head he wiped the moisture off the mirrors, clearing the messages away. He left the bathroom and knocked on Geordie to ask if he fancied going for a pint.

"Sure mate no worries let me grab me jacket." Geordie looked at Seb's face which had paled slightly and beads of sweat had come onto his forehead from being in the steamy bathroom.

"You alright mate; you look like you've just seen a ghost or somet."

Seb just gave him a lopsided grin.

"Yeah right, nah mate I'm good. Come on get ya jacket" Seb replied.

Crysta let the clouds close over the scene and smiled. That's my boy Seb, good lad.

Crysta then made a mental note to drop in her sister to tell her to look for a lad called Seb Tumble. If he called out of the blue then she may not listen to him. I'll just whisper in her ear when she's asleep like in Sixth Sense. That seemed to work well enough. Crysta smiled, they had already met but because of the whole dying thing before joining the Army, I wouldn't have met Seb to introduce him to her. I bet they get that feeling though, this will be interesting.

CHAPTER TWENTY-EIGHT

Crysta made her way to her the waiting room to find Gee throwing a stick for Prince. Crysta didn't even bother to enquire where the stick came from.

"Ah the wonderer returns. Did u get everything sorted?"

"Yep. Shall we do this then?"

"We! No we Crysta just you. I recommend the lift, the escalator requires shades. It takes almost forever and the choice of music on the way up isn't the best. The lift has a chair and a TV."

"Well that's a no brainer then, the lift it is." Crysta assumed stick throwing duty for Prince.

"Can Prince come, give me some company?"

"I think it's best you do it on your own. I'll get him back to Noah for you. You can pick him up later ok."

"Ok...um Gee."

"Yes."

"What do I say to him?"

"Say to who? Prince. Anything you want I'm sure he doesn't really understand you"

"No you idiot..God. What do I say to God. I mean he's God for crying out loud. This is huge. I mean I didn't really believe in him you know, but now he's going to be right there in front of me." Crysta was shaking her head in disbelief and had sunk into a chair as Prince dropped the stick at her feet, looking between her and the stick with imploring eyes.

"I normally find saying Hi, how are you? Is a good way to start a conversation."

"Very funny Gee."

"No I'm serious. Don't worry Crissy you'll be fine."

Crysta noted mentally how it was the first time Gee had called her Crissy. Well they had spent a lot of time together now so they were mates. He was a bit more relaxed around her now.

Crysta threw the stick for a very excited Prince who bounded through the clouds after it.

"Ok call the lift then."

"It's already here, enjoy the trip."

Crysta stepped through and had to push Princes nose out of the way of the doors as they closed shut. It was the best kitted out lift she had ever been in. Oh well may as well make the most of it. Crysta settled in the chair and turned on the telly. Going to the Vicar of Dibley episodes as most others before her normally did. It wasn't long however before Crysta soon drifted off to sleep. It had been a long day, or was it days. She had no idea of how long she had been up here. In her sleep Crysta's brain was replaying everything in reverse to try and organise the events so it could settle into a dreamless sleep. Too much had happened and Crysta slept fitfully in the chair, occasionally talking out loud. She was shouting at her sister as she sat in the audience at the Colin Fry show.

"Sky it's me Crysta, why can't you see or hear me...SKY!"

Sky was just sat there with a blank expression on her face not reacting to Crysta's shouts of her name.

CHAPTER TWENTY-NINE

"Hello"........... "Hello" Sky went to hang up the phone until she heard a hesitant

"Um hello, is this Sky?"

"Yes it is and who is this please?"

"Um my name is Seb I'm a friend of your sister Crysta."

"A friend of my sisters! Did you go to school together or something?"

"Not really no."

"Well where did you know her from then? Look if you're trying to get back in touch then I should inform you that she passed away about ten years ago."

"Yeah I know, it's you I would like to speak to. She gave me your number and asked me to get in touch."

"Who did?"

"Crysta"

"Hang on let me get this straight, my dead sister asked you to ring me."

"Yes, look can we meet face to face it's a long story."

"No I don't think so you're obviously some sort of weirdo."

"Please. Look you met me once. Your sister introduced us at a barbeque; you look a lot like your sister."

"Are you some kind of stalker watching me? Listen mate I'm in the Police and I can track this call and arrest you for harassment do you understand?"

"Please don't do that. This hasn't gone well at all. Look just ask me a question about your sister that I couldn't possibly know and if I get it wrong I won't bug you again, but if I get it right would you agree to meet me."

"I'm not sure let me think." As Sky paused on the phone her memory drifted to a weird dream she'd had. Her sister was telling her that a man called Tumble would ring and she needed to speak to him. Had she said Seb aswell?

"What did you say your name was again?"

"Seb"

"What's your surname? Is it something like Tumble?"

"No actually it's Dwyer but my friends, including your sister, call me Tumble. It's a nickname."

Her eyes almost bulged in her head. It was a dream wasn't it. No too weird. She took a breath.

"This is freaky. Ok then Seb or Tumble or whoever you are. Where and when do you want to meet?"

"Oh great you've had a change of heart. Can I ask why?"

"I think Crysta told me to expect a call from you, but I think it was a dream. I dunno I've been confused a lot lately. I feel like I only spoke to her the other day you know, Probably lack of sleep, or stress from my job."

"Do you really believe that? You know it was Crysta. Did she write on your mirror as well?"

"Say what now? No she just came to me when I was asleep."

"Oh she did the whole 'Ghost' thing with me and steamed up the mirrors in the block."

"Block?"

"Yeah, I'm in the Army. That's where I met your sister."

"Ok this is getting really mad now. Crysta was coming out of the Army careers office when she got hit by the car. She never made it into the Army." Sky hesitated "Yet I have this random memory of going to her pass out parade. This is giving me a headache. Look just give me your number and I'll give you a ring, I just need to get my head together ok. This call has been a bit much."

"Yeah, I understand. Speak soon then."

"Sure, Bye Seb." Sky hung up and sat back down into the chair that was next to the phone and stared disbelieving at the phone. It couldn't be possible but every fibre in her was screaming that it was right. Her sister didn't die but the only people that seemed to remember this were herself and Seb. Sky rang him straight back and arranged to meet him in a couple of days at Birmingham train station.

CHAPTER THIRTY

The lift bell woke Crysta and she wearily stepped out into a cloud.

I guess that is what Heaven is,' Crysta thought wearily,'a bloody big cloud with stuff floating in it.

As if to confirm her thoughts she could see a filing cabinet and a pretty looking secretary putting away some papers. Well Crysta assumed she was a secretary; she was wearing a conservative dark blue suit and glasses with her hair in a sensible bun. It's hard not to stereotype someone when they dress so obviously for their job. The lady noticed Crysta looking at her.

"Hello, you must be Crysta. I'm guessing your here to see the big G. If not you've made a long trip up here for nothing" She smiled at her own little quip.

"Yes I am" was all Crysta could say, slightly stunned that she had a Welsh accent.

"Ok no problems, just take a seat. Would you like a cup of tea or coffee?"

"Oh ok. Tea please, white, no sugar"

"White, no sugar. Does that mean milk no sugar? I don't really know that saying, I'm sorry. "

"Sorry, yes it does. Army thing I guess."

"You're in the Army. Oh how fascinating. I have great admiration for you guys, and girls of course."

"Thanks" Crysta liked the Welsh accent, especially how they could roll their R's.

"Is that how you, you know, you came to be up here? Get shot or something? In fact don't answer that it's not my place to pry. Anyway help yourself to the snacks over there. Remember you can't put on weight up here so pile your plate up. Right I'll go and get your Tea."

For the first time Crysta noticed the waiting area. Water fountain, white leather chairs and a long table covered in crisps and chocolate. Crysta walked over to inspect the goodies nearly walking into a chair.

Why make furniture white in a place where it's permanently white, Crysta wondered as she walked around the near invisible chair to inspect the table. It was strewn with all her favourites.

Makes sense, Crysta thought, I mean this is Heaven.

Crysta took a Snicker then put it back and picked up a packet of peanut M & M's. As they were the small packets she took a packet of Minstrels too, and then spotted the Maltesers. She stood with all three packets in her hand wondering which ones to have then she noticed the Aero bubbles. They had the mint and original.

"Oh no this is too hard." Crysta groaned out loud

"Here's your Tea Crysta."

"Oh thanks, you made me jump."

"Sorry about that."

"It's ok. I'm just having a chocolate dilemma. I like it all."

"Have as much as you want but you'll probably feel sick if you eat too much."

"Will I? I figured if I can't put on weight then I won't feel full or sick."

"Your brain hasn't accepted that yet. It will still tell your stomach that you've eaten too much. With time it'll realise you don't even need food at all. It's quite an adjustment, especially under the circumstances you came here under. I've just been reading your file. Interesting."

"Is it? Why what does it say?"

"This and that. You working with Sam, now that was intriguing."

"Not so much when you are actually working for him, more annoying."

"Really. Well I suppose he's not meant to be a nice guy."

Crysta just nodded her head in agreement.

"Keeping people hanging around with no soul just to recruit for him. Terrible. I can't even imagine what it's like not having a soul."

"It feels like nothing because you can't feel anything, but you so desperately want too. If that makes any sense."

"Sure, must have been awful. Oh well you're here now with soul intact" she said with what Crysta considered to be irritating perkiness.

"But I don't want to be here" Crysta blurted out.

"Excuse me?"

"I don't want to be here." Crysta said more under her breath this time.

"Oh love, how can you say that? You have everything you need by ere."

"I don't have my friends or family do I? There are people that I classed as mates that don't even remember me ever existing. I have family who believe I really did die when the car hit me, but it's not true."

"You should have died Crysta but Sam allowed you this extended time. You shouldn't have had it really. It's cruel but that's what he's about."

"I don't want to seem ungrateful. I'm confused. I hated not having a soul and working for him but at least I was with my friends and family. Now I'm just a memory, that's hard to deal with. I never had the chance to say goodbye properly."

"When most people die they don't get that luxury and you know that. You're just feeling sorry for yourself."

"Yeah I guess."

"What happened to you is unusual. We rarely get the good ones back off Sam once he has them. The Guv went out on a limb for you."

"I know" Crysta was looking glumly down at her hands.

"You still seem upset. Now tell me what would you rather. Being here, with your soul, and all that you could ever wish for. Bearing in mind your family and friends will join you again one day. It'll come around quicker than you imagine too. Years and months mean nothing here. Or go back down there soul less and under his control?"

"Down there I think. Ok working for Sam wasn't great but I sucked at the job anyway so I was pretty much free loading off the being able to stay around."

"How much longer do you think Sam would have put up with you being a dead weight on his resources Crysta before he got rid of you?"

"Dunno, he put up with me for ten years."

"Sure, but that is because he knew it annoyed the Guv. Now he knows the Guv has been able to take you back do you think he'd want you if you went back down there again anyway?"

"Probably not."

"Well I've gotta go we have a huge star that has just joined us. I'm a massive fan I can't wait to meet him. We haven't had anyone this big since Elvis. I'm hoping he's going to show me some of his famous moves like the Moonwalk. Of course it's Tom Jones I'm waiting for but It's a while yet until he's due. Well do you have all your questions sorted that you want to ask him? Most people want to know about death and destruction and the like. You know, why he lets bad things happen an that."

"I know why bad things happen, I worked for Sam remember! God can't win all the battles it's just when bad things happen to people it's hoping they have the faith to still believe in God because once they stop believing in him, Sam wins another member doesn't he."

"Very good Crysta."

"Yeah well I've had a while to think through stuff like that. I never used to believe in God before the accident you know. Ironic now, considering I'm sat in his waiting room"

"Hmmm yes. If you could ask him just one question then what would it be?"

Crysta thought for a moment "If he could send me back I guess."

"He has reincarnated people before but it's only under special circumstances."

"No I want to go back as me."

"You ask a lot Crysta, but good luck. I'll catch up with you later ok."

Once the secretary had disappeared into the cloud Crysta made her way over to the table and grabbed one of everything she could carry and placed them on the table next to her brew and munched her way through them until, as predicted, she felt sick. Crysta however didn't mind feeling sick on chocolate as it was a good kind of sick, satisfactory. Then she felt guilty but consoled herself that all the calories she just consumed weren't going to make a dent on her hips.

I hope that's true, Crysta observed looking at all the empty packets. I think that'll be another question I'll ask the Guv, just to make sure. If not I'm going to have to go for a run or somet.

CHAPTER THIRTY-ONE

"Wow you do look very similar. I was worried I wouldn't be able to recognise you. It's quite eerie really the similarity."

"Yeah I know. Sometimes we would be asked if we were twins. You know you do look like I have met you before."

"That's because you have."

Seb and Sky went quiet for a moment. They were sat in a Cafe by the station escalators.

"I don't remember. You said at a BBQ on the phone."

"It was at your parent's house. Crysta had invited me to stay the weekend to give me a break from the block. I was on the sofa of course."

"You guys weren't a couple then?"

"Not for the want of trying. I, unfortunately, was in the friend zone with Crysta. We've snogged n that you know, but she said it was weird coz I'm like a brother. I loved her though. Sorry love her."

"That's nice. I miss her desperately. I've had this feeling for a while that something wasn't quite right. What do the rest of your mates think about it? I daren't even mention this to my parents they'll think I'm nuts."

"I know what you mean. My mates don't even remember her. It's like the Men in Black came and wiped their memory of her. When I speak of her they say it's just me having a wet dream. Squaddies ay, always taking the mickey."

"Do you wonder why you still remember her then? I do."

"Yeah all the time. It must be for a reason though."

"I've been thinking about that and I was wondering if we're supposed to I dunno, summon her on a Ouija board or something."

"What? Are you kidding? Last time I mucked about with one of them things I think I nearly called up Hitler. No way, those things are dodgy if you don't know what you're doing."

"I do know what I'm doing. I promise. It's got to be worth a try don't you think?"

"I dunno Sky, seems a bit hocus pocus to me. I mean have you tried before to get her this way?"

"No, but bear in mind part of me remembers her dying ten years ago and another part of me remembers chatting to her on the phone the other day. It's all a bit confusing. It's like the memory of her wasn't erased properly and I've not got this conflicting information."

"For me it's more like she's an imaginary friend that's gone missing."

"So do you want to give it a go then?"

"What?"

"The Ouija board."

"I guess. I've got that scene from Bill and Ted in my head when they get called up by the step mum. Have you seen it?"

"Yep but I doubt it'll be like that."

"No I guess not. Lead the way then let's drop Crysta a line."

As they left to leave Seb asked,

"So how come you know about Ouija boards n that then? Is it because you're a bit of a hippy chick and you're also into Crystals and Tarot."

"Why do you think that I would be into Crystals and Tarot?"

"Well you know Ouija and your name is Sky."

"I didn't learn about Ouija because of my name and no I don't know anything about Tarot or crystals." Sky retorted a little irritably.

"Hey, sorry to offend."

"No it's fine sorry for snapping. I get questions like that a lot because of my name. I only know about Ouija because of a misspent youth messing around at sleepovers, that's all. One of my mates actually thought she was a white witch."

"Was she?"

"No but she was a really nice girl if not a little strange. She's probably a lawyer or something now."

They fell quiet as Sky mused and Seb well basically lost interest in the conversation and was thinking he might grab a pasty or something before they went back to Sky's place. Then it dawned on him. He was going back to Crysta's sister's house to use a Ouija board to try and speak to Crysta.

Things don't get more random than this, he realised.

CHAPTER THIRTY-TWO

St Peter had been summoned to the Guv's office.

"So how did it go with Crysta then Guv?"

"Not too bad. She's not happy by ere you know."

"Yes well there's no pleasing some people. You're speaking Welsh. Why are you speaking Welsh? Oh no, you didn't do your Welsh secretary thing again did you?"

"Yes. I only do it because people don't speak to me properly when I appear." was the non Welsh accent reply "I mean they either just sit there with their mouths opening and shutting like a fish out of water saying things like. You really exist, I always thought you did, or, you're exactly how I thought you would be. It gets very annoying after a while."

"Ok but why Welsh?"

"Well they call Wales God's country. I like that."

"Don't the Irish call it that also?"

"Possibly. Besides everywhere is, I made all of it. Anyway I can't do a good Irish accent."

"Ok so what did you want me for then Guv?" Peter asked trying to move away from the frivolous conversation.

"Like I said, Crysta isn't happy. She said she would rather be down there without her soul than up here. That doesn't make any sense to me."

"Did she say why she wasn't happy?"

"It's all because of her family and friends. It doesn't help that Jesus didn't do a very good job of adjusting her sister and Seb's minds and they still recollect being in contact with her after her supposed death. It makes things confusing for all of them."

"I did try and warn you about this. I said she may not appreciate being taken away from her family"

"Yes, yes I know I've made a mess of things this is why I've asked you to come up. What do you think I should do?"

St Peter stammered as he'd never been asked for advice by the Guv before.

"Well, um, you, you, see I do have an idea of how this can be resolved but it's completely against office policy. I mean if it got out that you did this you would have a queue outside your office a mile long."

"Really still I'm intrigued. Please Peter, do tell me this idea. Even though I have an idea of what you're about to say."

"Well I figured you would as you see and know all but I'll tell you anyway shall I?"

Once Peter had laid out his idea, God sat back in his chair deep in thought.

"You know" he finally said "That wasn't what I thought you were going to say at all but I like it. Get onto it and take Jesus with you."

"Me? You want me to go. But...but"

"No buts please Peter. It's your idea so I think you should be involved. Now off you pop there's a good chap. I've got a guest coming up soon."

"Wouldn't be the new superstar by any chance would it?"

"Well yes of course. You know I like to have one to one with everyone when they get here."

"I bet you don't show up as a Welsh secretary for him though" Peter whispered under his breath.

"What was that Peter?"

"Nothing Guv, just saying I'll be on my way."

"I'd like an e-mail about it once you're done."

"Yes Guv will do no problems." Peter put on his shades and left via the escalator. Anything to delay what he was going to do. Me and my big mouth, he shook his head miserably as he stood listening to 'He's got the whole world in his hands'.

....
....

Many hours later Jesus and Peter where stood in the visiting room.

"I can't believe he's making me do this."

"Well you did give him the idea."

"Yes I know but I still blame you."

"Me! Why me? What did I do?"

"You didn't sort it all out properly in the first place."

"Well A. I was in a bit of a rush and B. They have a real strong love for her. It's hard to mask that. Especially the sister as she never really accepted Crysta as being gone in the first place."

"Yes well, that may be the case but we must get it right this time."

"Ok fine." Gee swept his hand over and saw Seb and Sky were just about to start the séance after spending a few hours making the Ouija board out of whatever scrap paper Sky could find in the house.

"Shall we pretend to be Elvis or something?" Jesus asked giggling at what he thought would be a really funny thing to do.

"I don't think so do you; Elvis would go mad if he found out. Some of them can be quite tetchy about stuff like that."

"Well someone else then. Come on it'll be fun. Really mess with their heads."

"I don't think they need their heads any more messed up do you?"

"No you have a point. Let's do this then. You first."

"No you first, I insist."

"Don't be such a coward, it's not so bad down there."

"What are you talking about? You were scared stiff the whole time you were down there."

"No I wasn't!" Gee said defensively "Not the whole time. Maybe at first, but not all of the time I was down there. You get used to it after a while."

"Yes I'm sure you do. I personally don't plan to stay down there any longer than I need to thank you very much." With that he had stepped over the wall and was gone.

Jesus stood on the wall and dived bombed into the gap sending a puff of cloud streaming up and yelling "Geronimo!" as he went.

CHAPTER THIRTY-THREE

Crysta was getting bored of the chocolate and had decided to move onto the crisps when a cherub came out of nowhere and handed her a note.

Sorry to have kept you Crysta. I hope you have been enjoying the Buffet. I'm afraid I have been delayed. I will hopefully get to meet you again soon. Please use the express elevator. Press the red button on the wall to your left.

God

Oh great, Crysta thought as she watched the cherub waddle away. All the way up here for nothing. She looked at the Buffet and realised that it wasn't completely for nothing. Crysta went over to the red button.

It was shaped like a mushroom and had a sign above it saying Push. So she did.

Crysta started sinking into the clouds, as if she were in quick sand. Her instant thought was to panic and try and climb out onto solid ground. When she looked around she knew that was going to be difficult so she stood there. Her chin was now about where floor level was earlier and the cloud was moving slowly over her eyes. She closed them and she found she was now falling backwards through the clouds. Crysta felt like how Alice must have done when she fell down the rabbit hole. Her mind was whirring through everything, taking it into the past. Meeting Gee, walking Prince and taking the life from the deer. Still falling, another memory, it was Seb and the guys. Further back again: When she joined the Army. Even further: Leaving school and wanting to join the Army. The memory stopped there. She was stood outside the careers office. Crysta watched herself get hit by the car and the paramedics come. As she floated away from the scene she saw what looked very much like a cherub kicking what looked like a solicitor in the shins and trying to drag his briefcase away, trying to stop him from heading towards her. Then there was light, she shielded her eyes from the glare with her hand. Then there was nothing but white. Crysta felt like she had been swallowed by a marshmallow. Her head felt fuzzy.

Crysta sat up and looked around. She was lying on one of the sofa's outside the lifts to go up to the Guv's office. Prince the ever faithful dog had waited for her the whole time, took movement from Crysta to mean he could run over to her and lick her face. So he did, which certainly brought Crysta around quickly and she sat up sharply giving herself a head rush.

"Yuk Prince you dirty beast. I know where that tongue has been" she said wiping her face with her sleeve.

"Now where has Gee gone?" She looked around. Gee was just heading towards her.

"Hey pal what you been up to?"

"Not much. So how did it go then?"

"It didn't, I was blown out, he was busy or somet. I gorged out on the Buffet though. Then I must have drifted off because I had the maddest dream that I was falling and I saw when I had my accident. In fact it must have been a dream because I'm sure I saw a cherub trying to beat up some guy in a suit. Mental ay?"

"Yep, mental. Dreams tend to be a bit random though. Did you meet a Welsh secretary in the Guv's office?"

"Yeah she was nice. Told me I could eat what I want and not put on weight. Is that true? Coz if it is that would be awesome."

"You met him then."

"Who?"

"God"

"Nope not following. The secretary was God?"

"Yep"

"Shut up, no way. Are you serious?"

"Yeah, he does it quite a lot. He finds people don't speak openly and honestly with him when he is there being large and well, God like."

"Yeah I could see how that would happen. So let me get this straight. God likes to pretend to be a woman. Isn't that a form of cross dressing?"

"Are you saying God is a cross dresser. I don't think he'll appreciate that."

"Why do you think he heard me?"

"Uh yes! You've been here long enough to know that."

"Oops, Never mind. Hopefully he'll see the funny side. I suppose I should know I mean how long have I been here now?"

"About ten years isn't it?"

"Ten years! Really! Wow time flies up here. It only feels like a couple of days. Remind me later to check in on my sister. I think she has a new man in her life."

"Ok then. Crysta, check in on your sister later. There done."

"Not very helpful Gee, not very helpful at all."

"Yeah, but funny."

"Only to you Gee. Something is only funny when another person finds it funny and not just yourself. Anyway enough chat I want to get a shower, clean my teeth and a change of clothes. I feel disgusting like I've been in these clothes for ages." She paused. "Now which way is it?"

"This way, the same way it's been for the past ten years."

"Yeah sure of course. Lose my head if it weren't screwed on. Well it all looks the same, it can be confusing sometimes."

"Well you have plenty of time to get used to it. You know you don't actually need to shower and that anymore don't you?"

"I know but it makes me feel better. Why don't you shower?"

"No"

"Uh gross. I'm going to call you stinks from now on."

"But I don't smell."

"I'll take your word for that. Don't be walking too closely stinks." She turned to look over her shoulder "Come on Prince lets go."

With that they disappeared into the clouds.

CHAPTER THIRTY-FOUR

Sky didn't normally stop to eat in a cafe at the station when she came off shift. She didn't like being in her uniform when she wasn't on duty. Today though a chocolate muffin had caught her eye and she figured a quick choc stop wouldn't hurt.

She hadn't long sat down when a man about her age came over.

"Uh hey. Sorry to interrupt you but my wallet has just been stolen."

Sky groaned inwardly. Another reason for not wearing uniform when off shift, people didn't know you were off shift.

"Ok give me your details" she said getting out her notebook.

Seb gave her his number and turned to give the lads a thumbs up. Sky looked up in time to notice him doing this.

"Have you really lost your wallet sir?" Sky asked coldly.

Seb turned around to look at Sky. "Uh no, it was a dare, sorry. The guys said I wouldn't be able to get you to take my phone number."

Sky looked over her shoulder at the group of lads that were trying not to give her eye contact.

"Did they indeed? Well you did, so well done."

"That's my real number if you want to, I dunno get together."

"Ok, not only did you just waste police time you are now trying to pick me up."

"Yes, how am I doing?"

Sky just had a feeling that the reason she had taken this out of character pit stop was so she would meet him. Her sister was playing her games again. Sky shook her head and smiled. Even when she had died Sky had always felt her around her and this had a feel of Crysta about it. Crysta must want her to meet him.

"Would you like to join me or are you and your friends off to a pub?"

"Well yes I would love to join you. Just give me a second to let the guys know what the score is."

Seb tried to walk nonchalantly over to where Smudge, Geordie and Lurch were stood. They were doing a bad job of trying to look inconspicuous.

"Well mate, how did you do? Looks like a result from here." Geordie noted.

"She's asked me to join her and she took my number."

"Get in mate" was Smudge's comment.

"Up close she looks familiar like I've met her before. Does she look familiar to you guys? We haven't been arrested by her or something when we've been drunk?"

They all stared and Sky noticing the scrutiny just gave them a quick wave.

Suddenly their eyes were diverted quickly back onto Seb.

"Well?" Seb enquired.

"No, but she's quite fit mind."

"Cheers Geordie. Your right though. I'll have a coffee or somet with her and catch up with you guys in about half an hour or so ok."

"Maybe she's a famous person who is pretending to be a copper" Lurch suddenly interjected into the conversation.

"I don't think so Lurch do you? Right you lot scarper I'll text you to find out where you are ok."

"I canna believe your baling out on us for a woman so soon man, that's poor."

"Are you trying to tell me Geordie that if it was the other way around you wouldn't? Anyway you sent me over there."

"Yeah but to be fair we didn't think you would get anywhere mate."

"Cheers Smudge. Look you lot scarper I'll catch up soon I promise. I can't let you guys get too many pints ahead of me can I?"

"All reet. See you later then."

"Laters guys." Seb turned away and headed back to the table where Sky had been watching the whole episode with interest.

"So are you just starting shift or just finishing?"

"Just finished. I normally go straight home after shift and get the uniform off, because people like you normally come over and annoy me."

"So why didn't you go straight home today then?"

"I saw this chocolate muffin and" Sky paused "and, I dunno. I just think Crysta wanted me to be here." Sky realised she had said it out loud and flushed slightly with embarrassment knowing what question was coming next. This guy is going to think I'm nuts, Sky thought, so she quickly jumped in with a question to hopefully divert him away.

"Sorry I didn't catch your name. I'm Sky."

Seb extended his hand. "Seb. Did I hear you say something about a person wanted you here?"

"I was hoping you had missed that."

"Really! Why? Who is Crysta?"

"My sister."

"Oh ok."

"She passed away about ten years ago."

"Okay" was all Seb could say.

"I know you think I'm crazy now don't you?"

"No not really."

Sky looked sceptical. Seb continued.

"No really, I think I've seen a ghost before. I believe in them."

"Seems weird speaking to you about her, I've only just met you."

"So you said that you feel that Crysta wanted you to be here."

"Sounds mad I know but I've always felt her around me. My parents too sometimes and when things happen out of the ordinary we, I don't know, we just assume its Crysta. That Crysta is helping us out and watching over us. It's comforting."

"How did she die?"

"She got hit by a car. She had literally just signed on for the Army too. She was only seventeen."

"Sorry that sucks. I'm in the Army."

"Are you! Woh. So were the rest of ya pals squaddies too?" In her mind Sky was thinking that Seb being in the Army was just too much of coincidence.

"Yeah. Just having a lads night out."

"Well I'll let you get back to your friends. I have your number I'll be in touch ok."

"I don't suppose I could have your number as well could I?"

"Sure." Sky got her notebook out again and scribbled it down. "I'm going to get out of this uniform. Take care Seb I'm sure we'll catch up again soon. Enjoy your night and be good. I don't want to hear of any of my colleagues needing to pick you up."

"I'm always good Sky, I promise. I'll ring soon ok."

"Sure ok, take it easy." Sky walked away telling herself not to look back when her mobile beeped. It was a text from a yet to be registered caller.

Miss u already. Seb

Sky smiled and turned but Seb had gone. She saved the number and grinned.

Nice one Crysta, he's not too bad at all.

Crysta closed the gap up in the clouds and grinned.

"He seems nice Gee. I reckon I would have got on with him"

"I'm sure you would. Are you coming then?"

"Yeah two secs, I just wanna check in on the folks then I'll be right with ya"

"Cool….Uh Crysta. Do you like it here?"

Crysta looked up from what she was doing.

"Sure Gee. What's not to like. I can eat what I want without getting fat and I can speak to loadsa famous people that I would have never have got to meet while I was alive. Why do you ask?"

"No reason, just asking that's all. I'll meet you in the bar ok"

"Ok. Cool. See you in a bit. Hey Gee that is another good thing, underage drinking."

"Like you weren't doing that down there anyway. Besides you are technically twenty seven now."

"Yeah good point. I suppose never getting old is a bonus. I've noticed my sister's hair is going a bit grey. Do you think I should leave her some hair dye on the side or something?"

"Your sister can figure that out for herself, she doesn't need you to intervene in everything."

"Yeah I suppose."

"See you in a bit then."

"Yeah bye."

Gee walked away feeling very pleased. It had been tricky, especially with Peter moaning throughout the whole operation, but it had been a success.

He headed off to e-mail the Guv the news.

The Guv himself obviously already knew and was in the middle of e-mailing Sam. It simply read....

In your face Sam! LOL.

He signed it off with a smiley face giving the bird.

THE END

TO JESUS,
I HOPE THIS BOOK
HELPS.
FM
GOD

THE BOOK OF ARMY SLANG AND SAYINGS
& other useful info

Phonetic Alphabet – Used in radio procedure

A = ALPHA
B = BRAVO
C = CHARLIE
D = DELTA
E = ECHO
F = FOXTROT
G = GOLF
H = HOTEL
I = INDIA
J = JULIET
K = KILO
L = LIMA
M = MIKE
N = NOVEMBER
O = OSCAR
P = PAPA
Q = QUEBEC
R = ROMEO
S = SIERRA
T = TANGO
U = UNIFORM
V = VICTOR
W = WHISKY
X = XRAY
Y = YANKEE

24 HOUR CLOCK

1pm = 1300hrs	7pm = 1900hrs
2pm = 1400hrs	8pm = 2000hrs
3pm = 1500hrs	9pm = 2100hrs
4pm = 1600hrs	10pm = 2200hrs
5pm = 1700hrs	11pm = 2300hrs
6pm = 1800hrs	12pm = 0000hrs (midnight)

RANK STRUCTURE

RANK	DESCRIPTION	SLANG NAME
Private (Pte)*	No rank	NIG, TOM, FNG, Sprog *
Lance Corporal (LCpl)	One chevron	Lance jack
Corporal	Two chevrons	Full screw
Sergeant (Sgt)	Three chevrons	Sarge, Sossarge
Staff Sergeant (SSgt)	Three chevrons & a crown	Staff, Staffie
Warrant Officer 2 (WO2)	A large crown	Sir, woh two, prick with a stick
Warrant Officer 1 (WO1)	A large crown encircled with a laurel leaf	Sir, woh one, prick with a stick

Please note: Everyone below Sergeant are known as Junior non-commissioned officers (JNCO'S) Sergeants and above are Senior non-commissioned officers (SNCO'S)

Everyone above WO1 are Officers known as Sir or Maam.

All none Army people are just civilians (Civvies)

*Private can change depending on Regiments i.e. Signals - Siggies. Engineers – Sapper Artillery – Gunner. Infantry – Rifleman.

* Translations in the dictionary

TRANSLATIONS AND SAYINGS

ASAP – As soon as possible.

Basic – As in Basic training. The ten week course you need to pass to be classed as a basic Soldier.

Bergen – A large Army rucksack

Beasting – Being made to do physical exercise until death feels like a better option

Block – Another name for the accommodation for JNCO's

Bomb burst – Leave, as in, 'Before you bomb burst'

Brew – Tea or coffee

CBRN – Chemical, Biological, Radiological, Nuclear

Chick – A female

Circuits – Physical training using varied times and different pieces of equipment

Cookhouse – Where JNCO's eat

Cooking on gas – Doing really well

FNG – F**king new guy

Feet in my In tray – If this is said to you by a higher rank it means you're in trouble

Gas, Gas, Gas – A phrase shouted into your Respirator to push out any gas that may have seeped into your mask

Gagging – Really desperate for- Normally a brew or a beer

Grannified – Looking like an old Granny

Guchi – Means really good

Hanging out of their hoop- So tired during exercise that they need all available orifices to help them breath

Head sheds/honchos – The people in charge

Hit the ground running – No time to think about what you're about to do

It's your train set – You're in charge run things as you want

Minging – Really drunk

NAAFI – Navy, Army, Air force Institute. Where JNCO's go for a break, scoff and alcohol

NIG – New in guy

Permanent send – Means a person is either talking too much or they are inadvertently holding down the pressle switch on their radio and are sending without meaning too

Pop smoke – Leave (See Bomb burst) derived from what happens when you throw a grenade

PTI – Physical training instructor

Pull – To go on the pull is to go out looking for a partner

Quite fit – A description of a person who is good looking but not necessarily physically fit

RAF – Royal Airforce

Rag week – Another way of describing a woman when it's their time of the month

Respirator – Mask worn when doing CBRN training

Sack it – To stop doing something

Scoff /Scran – Food

Spanner – Meant as an insult implying the person is stupid

Spitting feathers – Meaning your mouth is dry and you need a drink

Sprog – New guy just out of Basic training

Stag on – Is said to a person who is working when you are not and are normally about to go out and drink

Singing off the same song sheet – To make sure everyone is at the same understanding

Stingy – Tight with money

Squaddies – Soldiers

Tab – Forced speed march carrying weight

Teach anyone to suck eggs – Tell you your job

Thin out – Leave (See bomb burst)

Whole new ball game – Should something go wrong it changes things

About the Author

Nikki Shepherd currently lives in Wiltshire (Where all the best writers come from, like Terry Pratchett) She lives in Salisbury with her two dogs and husband Andy.

Nikki has been in the Army over twelve years and has the nickname of Vinny.

Nikki got the idea for Crysta while out walking one of her pet dogs. Rather than just forget about it, she did what most people say they would like to do but never actually get around to doing, and wrote a book.

Lightning Source UK Ltd.
Milton Keynes UK
15 July 2010

157063UK00001B/55/P